A SNEAKY IN...

OPERATION

DIAMOND ◇ FALL

A 10 - 16
CHRISTIAN SPY
ACTION-ADVENTURE!

BOOK 2

ROB BADDORF

Operation Diamond Fall:
A 10 - 16 Christian Spy Action-Adventure!
Book 2 in
A Sneaky Inc. Spy Adventure

Jar Of Lightning
Camp Hill, PA 17011
jaroflightning.com

ISBN: 978-1-956061-56-7

Written by
Rob Baddorf

Okay, so Robin had lied to her.

To Isabella. She asked who was on the other end of the walkie-talkie, and Robin straight-up lied.

He honestly didn't see why it was all that big a deal. After all, he lied for *her* own good. Who was Marlin Ledger to her? Nobody. Just some guy who was overdue his day in federal court.

So then why did it still bother him, weeks later?

Robin pressed the thoughts back down. Back under the rug, so to speak. This wasn't the time to deal with them. He had to focus on what was important. Not on these silent thoughts. Not on the whispers in his mind.

Robin glanced at the sunset. Stunning. The blending of hues made for a watercolor sky.

Pulling on his face mask, Robin looked up. The tallest ladder he had ever seen loomed above him. A true stairway to heaven.

Robin didn't like heights, never had. Something about being high up made him feel out of control. Like he was at the mercy of something else. Something he couldn't trust. Gravity?

Robin and Chad had snuck into the Empire Hotel construction site. After the team scouted the area and tracked the workers' routines over the last week, now was the time to take advantage of all that intel. Sneaking into the site was easy. A few snips, and the boys slipped under the barbed wire fence.

Now came the fun part.

Or, if you had any amount of healthy fear of heights, the *not*-so-fun part.

KR-CLINK!

An oversize padlock thumped to the ground in a plump of dust. No longer needing the blowtorch, Chad tossed it behind a few bags of concrete. Then he swung open the security gate barring the entrance to the towering crane.

"I just need to say," Chad whispered from under his own mask, "I have *always* wanted to climb up one of these construction cranes. I mean, do you have any idea just how high up we're going to be?"

Robin didn't know. And everything inside of him told him he didn't *want* to know either.

"Two hundred and sixty-five feet. Ha! Can you believe it?" Chad said as he began scrambling upward. "That's as tall as a twenty-six story building."

Besides the bright red hard hat, Chad had on his "business uniform": black pants, black shirt. Tight-fitting, so that nothing could get snagged. And he wore latex gloves, so he didn't leave any fingerprints behind. On the first mission with Chad, the kid almost couldn't talk about anything else except how weird the gloves felt. Somehow, Chad had convinced himself that he was allergic to them. He itched all night. It turned out he wasn't allergic to the latex, like most normal people. He was allergic to the thin layer of talcum powder inside. Go figure.

Chad handled the rungs of the ladder like he was a natural. He sprinted up the first set of rungs like a monkey. And since Chad hadn't hit his growth spurt yet, his easy scampering only made him look even more like a kid on a playground. All except for his bent ears. The tips of them folded down. Don't they say if you hold your eyes crossed for too long, they'll stay that way? Did Chad get bored and hold the tips of his ears down for too long?

Robin looked around him.

The construction site was empty. Just like they had observed every night that week.

He took in a deep breath and climbed the first rung. Were his hands already sweating?

Now he only had two hundred and sixty-four rungs remaining!

2

ROBIN WANTED TO THANK whoever invented the rest platforms on a construction crane. He didn't need the break to catch his breath, as much as to have something solid to put his feet on again.

"Hurry up!" Chad yelled from somewhere above. "You have to see the view from up here!"

Robin had already closed his eyes. He didn't want to see the view. Right now, he wanted the wind to stop. He could feel the giant tower swaying side to side. The movement made him feel seasick. Who would have thought he needed to pack Dramamine? Robin tried to will the crane to stop moving.

"From my vantage," a voice said in Robin's earpiece, "it looks like you're in last place."

It was Isabella. She must have a pair of binoculars trained on Robin and Chad. She operated out of the trailer, disguised as a lawn-mowing service, that Sneaky, Inc. had equipped with all their high-tech gear.

Robin touched his earpiece. "Wanna switch places?"

"No. Not exactly."

"Ha! Then how about a little grace, will you? This is really high up," Robin said, opening his eyes. The view *was* amazing. He could see the city stretched out in front of him. The streetlights blinked on like little train models. Cars hardly looked like they were even moving from this height. And the people? They were almost too small to see. The feeling of vertigo twisted Robin's gut. He turned his head upward, choosing to focus on something above him instead. A single star had come out early.

"Grace? What do you mean by that?" came the response. "I thought that was what ballerinas had. You know, they're graceful."

"That's different," Robin said with a grin. He was happy for the distraction. "The grace I'm referring to is when you get something you don't really deserve. Something good, like a second chance."

"A second chance? Wait. Is this more of your God stuff?"

Robin laughed. "Yeah, I guess. If you ever think you need that kind of grace, I'll be glad to tell you more."

"Ah, thanks." There was another pause. Longer. "But no thanks."

"Okay. Back to work then." Robin shut off his mic. With all of his diversions gone, he had to climb again. This operation had better be worth it.

"How you doing down there, boss?" Chad suddenly poked his head over the landing above. "You look kinda sick."

Robin thought about a response.

Tell him the truth.

It was one of those whispers again. Not exactly in his head. Maybe more like in his heart. He didn't know. It was too hard to pinpoint.

"I'm doing great, Chad. I just have a . . . uh . . . a cramp in my side, that's all," Robin replied. At least that was mostly true. If he thought about it, he could practically imagine a side cramp coming on.

Hand over hand, Robin began the last set of rungs near the top.

"Hey, I was wondering if you would take a photo of me once you get up here? You know, one of those shots that stupid kids take of themselves hanging off something stupidly high up?"

"Chad, are you trying to join the stupid kids' club or what?" Robin focused on the next rung. And then the next. He could do this. Of course, Chad wasn't painting pretty pictures in Robin's mind. He really didn't want to envision what Chad was saying too closely. But then again, the conversation was offering something new to focus on. "No. I won't take a photo of you hanging off the edge."

"Oh, I know it's foolish. But can you imagine how many likes I'd get on social media? I mean, wouldn't that almost make it worth it? Wait, you think I should hang and take a selfie instead?"

"In case you were actually serious . . . no," Robin said, finally arriving at the top platform. His breathing sounded labored.

Chad shuffled out of the way, giving Robin a good view of the operator's shack. It almost looked like a cramped tollbooth sitting at the top of the world. It wasn't large. Just enough space for one adult to work in.

A gentle breeze blew. Robin clutched the rail with both hands. The platform was hardly wide enough for the two of them. Robin focused his eyes on the door to the operator's cabin. He wished he had actually brought blinders. Anything to block the view of nothing but empty air out of the corners of his eyes!

Robin had to focus. They could do this!

Chad unzipped a small case, slipping out a set of wafer-thin lock-picks. He carefully inserted them into the cabin door handle. Just as his fingers began the delicate work, the wind suddenly picked up. Chad hunched in closer to protect the doorknob, but it wasn't enough.

Robin gripped the handrail tighter. He was fine. Everything was fine. This was all part of the plan.

"Hey, can you block the wind for me?" Chad asked, trying to get a better grip on his fragile tools.

Robin slid in closer. He tried to turn his body to shelter Chad and the door, but he didn't want to let go. The railing was his only protection. And the wind seemed to come from every direction. Robin couldn't figure out where to position himself. Maybe if he just let go with one hand, he could—

A stronger gust of wind whistled past.

The entire tower swayed, rocking the precarious crane nearly four feet from side to side.

Instinctively, Robin returned his hand to the railing. Both of his hands white-knuckled the metal.

Which momentarily left Chad unprotected.

The lockpicks rattled and slipped out of the door's lock—

And fluttered away!

3

"OH, GREAT!" CHAD YELLED. "Now look what you made me do!"

"Me?! Why is it always my fault?"

"You need to start listening to more audiobooks while you work, Robin. There's a classic book called *From Good to Great*. You should give it a listen. In it, the author talks about Level Five Leadership. A good leader would suck it up and take ownership of the problem. And that owner would be *you*, in case you didn't know it."

"Since when did you start listening to business books?"

"Do you have any idea how long the library waitlist is to listen to Harry Potter?"

"Well, don't you have another set of lockpicks?" Robin tried to get back on topic.

"Yes. But they're at home. On my basement workbench. And if you haven't looked around recently, those aren't going to help us up here."

Rats. Robin knew about best-laid plans and how they always went awry. This didn't have to be a major problem. They just had to stay flexible. Robin merely had to relax. Relax, and give his fingers a rest from choking the handrail.

Robin eased up his grip and hunched down to lower his center of gravity.

"Oh, I've got it," Chad said, suddenly standing. "Duh. I'll just break the glass." He pulled his arm back, away from the window. And then, with one swift move, he swung his elbow forward, hitting the glass.

BONK!

Chad's elbow bounced off the reinforced glass. "Ow, ow, ow!"

Surely one of them had packed a hammer, hadn't they? Robin rummaged through his backpack. Nothing.

"Should I try hitting it again? This time I could try a headbutt."

"No, no. We need to keep as many of the brain cells that you have left, Chad. But thank you."

Robin zipped up his pack again. They could do this. No sweat. Breaking into a garden shed that hovered two hundred feet above the ground couldn't possibly be all that tricky, could it? Robin wiped away the sweat growing on his forehead.

"Oh, look," Chad said, poking at the large window. "The crane operator drinks diet Dr Pepper!"

"CHAD! How is that important right now?!"

"Well, it might be important if you were thirsty yourself, and if you were looking for a no-calorie drink that was both refreshing and bubbly all at the same time. Which, right now, would be me!"

Robin tilted his head back. He needed more oxygen flowing to his brain. More ideas and insight to get inside the—

"Wait a minute," Robin said, his head lowering. "If the crane operator drinks diet Dr Pepper, then maybe it's because he's thirsty. And what if he's thirsty because he's hot?"

"I'm not sure where you're going with this. Except you're making me *more* thirsty."

"I'm talking about air. The guy's gotta be able to open and close a window when it gets hot, doesn't he?"

Chad and Robin began examining the window's edges, looking for cracks or a way to wedge it open.

"It's gotta be boiling hot in there when the sun is out. How does the crane operator stay cool?"

And there it was.

4

AN AIR CONDITIONER HUNG out the back of the crane operator's shed.

Robin inched his way to it. There wasn't as much platform to stand on there. When he glanced down, the distance was staggering. Robin had to close his eyes for a moment to keep from tossing his dinner.

"Phillips," Robin whispered, with his hand outstretched.

Chad slapped the screwdriver into his palm. Robin got to work as fast as he could. One after another, he extracted the screws that held the AC unit in place.

It really wasn't a big deal, was it? What he had told Isabella. He was making the whole thing into a bigger deal than it was. He figured he would just tell her the truth later on. When it was a better time. It wouldn't be difficult to explain his reasons for bending the truth in the moment.

After all, in the business of working with the FBI, sometimes it was good to *not* know everything. Robin's handlers never told him all the details. Just what he needed to know for the mission. He was fine with that. He didn't want to know too much. In fact, it wouldn't surprise Robin if the FBI had already lied to him. That was fine too. That was the cost of doing this kind of business . . . wasn't it?

Anyway, it didn't matter. Why was he still consumed with something that wasn't an issue?

The last screw fell out. With his other hand, Robin allowed the AC unit to gently tip backward into his arms. It wasn't a full-size unit—maybe half the size of a normal window unit. But Robin had also never removed an AC unit at two hundred feet in the air. He cradled the box and slowly lowered it. Now would *not* be a good time to lose his footing.

Fortunately, Robin didn't run into any problems as he set the unit on the shrinking platform.

He relaxed just a bit. "You're up."

With Chad being as small and skinny as he was, he was the obvious candidate to squeeze through the opening. Robin just hoped that Chad wouldn't complain. Because there was *no way* Robin would do it.

"You wanna know a cool piece of trivia?" Chad eagerly threw himself into the open hole, his legs kicking and flailing behind him. "There's no bathroom in these tower cranes. Did you know that?"

"No, I can't say that I did."

"If they have to go number one, they just pee in a bottle." Chad had nearly his entire body inside the cab now. "Guess what they do if they have to go number two."

"No, thank you."

Chad suddenly stood up inside the glass-covered shack. With a flick of the lock, he opened the tiny door. "Wait, you don't want to know?"

"Not really," Robin said as he squeezed inside. It was cramped. There was almost no place to stand. Chad had to sit up on the back of the crane operator's seat to make room for Robin to sit in the chair properly.

Chad continued. "What if you're on a game show someday? And they offer you a million dollars if you know the answer."

Robin glanced back over his shoulder. "Then I guess I'm out of luck." Turning back around, he tapped his earpiece. "Check, check. The eagle has landed, over."

"Roger that," Isabella said in his earpiece. "Tell me when you've got that thing up and running."

"What if we get stuck up here and you have to go?" Chad asked. "Are you gonna want to know then?"

Doing his best to ignore Chad, Robin scanned the controls in front of him. Dials and buttons littered the dashboard.

A large button displayed: START.

Robin pressed it.

The giant crane engine coughed and spit. Out of the side mirrors, Robin spied a plume of black smoke erupting from the exhaust pipes.

The engine roared to life!

Robin placed a finger on his earpiece. "Isabella, you are my eyes now." He lifted his finger again.

"So, you'd just hold it? Is that what you're telling me?"

"Chad, can we please change the topic?"

"That depends," Chad said, kicking the seat. "Oh, wait . . . I just gave you the answer."

5

Isabella's voice came in bold and strong. "Alright, using the left control stick, move the crane twenty-three point five degrees to the south."

"I see the left control stick," Robin said. "Which way is south?"

"Um . . . to your left."

Robin gently pressed on the joystick. Sure enough, the giant boom arm inched to the side. It was working—actually moving! And it was *sooo* much fun!

"Oops, no, wait! Sorry. The *other* left."

Robin corrected the mistake. He couldn't believe it took so little effort to move something this gigantic. He watched as the boom arm slowly drifted to the right. Maybe if this FBI job didn't work out, Robin could become a crane operator.

Then he remembered the ladder climb. Okay, maybe not.

Robin could feel a tapping behind him. Chad's foot kept a steady beat that felt more like impatience. "Hey, when do I get to drive this thing?!" Chad finally barked.

"Chad, what are you talking about? We're sticking to the plan. Five more degrees and we're done."

But Chad must not have liked the answer. That or maybe he wasn't even listening, because he suddenly lunged for the controls.

"I just want to try it!"

Crushing Robin in the process, Chad lost his footing and slipped. He hit several joysticks at once, causing the engine to abruptly roar louder! The long crane arm lurched to the side. The giant hook dangling at the end appeared to stay in place. But when the motion finally rippled down to it, the hook swung dramatically.

Robin shoved Chad back into his place. "Look what you've done!"

"I'm—I'm so sorry!"

Both boys watched on in horror as the six-foot-tall crane hook continued to gain speed, swinging wildly from center. How much did that hook weigh? A thousand pounds? Two thousand?!

The hook finally slowed . . . slowed . . . coming to a stop.

Only that's when it swung back in the other direction.

Toward the skyscraper under construction.

It swung like a freight train in slow motion.

Robin had to do something. If he didn't, the hook would smash through the wall of glass windows!

6

Robin tried to time it. Like stopping a swinging ball on a string. He moved the joystick slowly, and then more steadily. He tried to counteract the swing of the hook.

The solid steel hook whipped through the air.

Closer . . . closer . . .

At the very last second, Robin jerked the controls, tugging the crane arm away from the building.

The hook slowed, getting still closer.

Slowing . . .

And then kissed the wall of glass—

Barely missing it—

Before it swung away.

"Phew," Chad breathed, leaning back. "That was close. I just wanted a chance to drive this thing. I mean, I did pretty good with the armored truck, am I right? You remember that, don't you?"

"Yes, I do remember," Robin growled. "But you could have asked instead of climbing over me!"

"Yeah. I'm sorry. Boy, that was scary there for a second." Chad sighed. "Now I wish they *did* have a bathroom up here."

With the hook coming to a stop, Robin continued to inch the crane arm toward its destination. "Thank you. Too much information."

"Yeah, okay. I can hold it."

Robin pressed his earpiece. "Twenty-three point five degrees, completed."

"Did you get a little excited there?" Isabella asked. "From down here, it looked like someone was having a bit too much fun."

"Yeah, something like that."

"Alright, you're over the museum now. Lower the hook block, and you're good to go."

"Roger that. Over and out." Robin studied the hand controls. Thankfully, someone had clearly marked them. Robin pressed a new joystick, watching the hook block slowly lower.

"This is going to be the best part, you know?" Chad said, wiggling his way back out of the AC hole.

"Yeah," Robin said, hitting the OFF switch on the tower crane. The engine rumbled and gargled for a bit. Eventually, it gave up the fight, stopping dead. Robin opened the door and joined Chad out on the crane arm. Robin couldn't help but look down again. The height they were at was incredible! His hands shook.

"The best part, huh?" Robin said, swallowing hard. "Right."

7

CHAD STOOD OUT OVER the trolley that held the giant hook far below. Did that boy have absolutely no fear of heights? He seemed as comfortable as he would have been standing on the ground.

Chad uncoiled the steel cable from his harness and clipped himself in.

This wasn't a zipline where you slid toward one side. This was a descent straight down. And it was "only" some two hundred feet to the museum roof below.

Robin yanked off his latex gloves. Drying his hands on his pants, he slipped on a pair of thick leather gloves.

Did he really want to watch how Chad did this? Would that be helpful or not?

Chad turned toward Robin and, with a salute, clutched his heart, pretending to be shot.

Robin watched as Chad allowed himself to "die" before falling off the edge.

Okay, not helpful.

Chad's cabling jerked, catching him. With a big smile and a thumbs-up, Chad began his controlled descent.

Now it was Robin's turn.

He inched forward, out onto the crane's arm. Was the wind picking up again? Robin had to force his muscles to continue working. One foot in front of the other. It wasn't far now.

A gust of wind pushed against the crane, causing the long arm to sway.

Robin grabbed ahold of the metal trusses, his knuckles whitening.

Everything was alright. Everything was just fine. Normal.

Somewhere, long ago, Robin had learned how to lie to himself. Somehow, it made things alright again. Even if they really weren't.

Robin forced one of his hands to let go. As quickly as he could, he reached for his safety harness clip. But his hands continued to shake. He couldn't get a good grip.

Robin had to focus on what was in front of him. But the distance between the cable before him and the glass-covered museum far below messed with his head. Robin was pretty sure the phenomenon was called parallax. All a matter of your point of view.

Sorta like truth and lies.

Another burst of wind suddenly blew. The entire four-hundred-thousand-pound tower twisted and groaned. Metal screeched against metal.

KR-CLICK!

Robin had just connected his harness clip to the central steel cable—

When he lost his grip!

8

Anika wove her way through a busy industrial kitchen. She carried a large tub of uncut onions.

She wore a crisp, clean food preparer's uniform. Charcoal gray, double-breasted with buttons mirrored on both sides. Her frizzy hair was pulled back tight and tucked under a matching gray hat.

The caterers for the gala were short-staffed. Especially when a bad bisque soup several days earlier had taken out some of their staff. Food poisoning—nothing too serious.

This left room for Anika. She had done all the research and taken all the interviews. Aced them, if you asked her. And even more conveniently, Anika just happened to be available to work on the night of the gala. Her new boss couldn't have been more pleased. He couldn't stop grumbling about needing all the help they could get. Especially with an event so large, and a menu so demanding. Who scheduled something like this with such short notice?

Anika whisked past a chef chopping Matsutake mushrooms. Another fileted a white fish of some sort.

Anika's supervisor had assigned her onions. Loads of onions. A whole bin of the wretched things! All for a classy version of French onion soup. Anika was *not* getting paid enough for this job.

She arrived at her tiny, cramped work station. A cutting board and one sharp knife awaited her.

Anika would NOT be cutting onions if she didn't also happen to be working a second job that same evening. A job involving an unmentionable group of fourteen-year-olds and an unnamed top secret organization.

Anika sighed, slicing into her first onion.

A waft of stinging vapor twisted upward. She shut her eyes—if only for a moment—trying to prevent the inevitable.

As fiery tears formed in her eyes.

9

ROBIN WAS IN A free fall.

He was tethered to the central cable, but he couldn't tell which end was up. Everything was a blur. His body tumbled through air. The wind ripped past him at an alarming speed. His face mask tore off. Without his face protection, his eyes watered. Robin was blind.

Weightlessness felt weird. His stomach lifted, making him sick. Out of control. His feet ached to feel solid metal beneath them again. Only, his feet were now above the rest of him.

Instinctively, Robin reached out, his arms flailing. If only he could grasp something to slow his descent! Something real and solid.

And that's when he brushed it.

The central cable.

Robin grabbed for it. Once he had a lifeline to tell up from down, Robin quickly righted himself. Both hands vice-gripped the thick cable. The friction was unbelievable. But his leather gloves took most of the damage.

His body slowed. His descent was now manageable. And to his own surprise, Robin gently alighted on the hook block next to Chad.

Silence.

Chad lifted his own mask. "Wow, I'm jealous. I didn't know that was an option. Tell me that was planned and a load of fun!"

With his heart hammering inside his chest, Robin suddenly noticed a new pain. His hands burned! Robin flung off both gloves like they were on fire. The central cable now provided some cool relief to his bare palms.

"Planned?" Robin responded, clearing his throat. "Um, sure. Something like that."

"I'm gonna do that next time. Seriously, it looked super cool from here. I can only imagine how it felt to actually do that. I didn't know that was your kinda thing, Robin."

Robin forced a grin. "Hang around me enough," he said, trying to hide his shaking hands, "and you'll learn a thing or two."

"I guess so. Go figure. I didn't take you for a daredevil."

The boys only had about a dozen feet left to go to the museum's rooftop. As Chad hooked up a short rope to the hook block, Robin took a breather. Peering beneath them cautiously, he spied growing activity at the front of the museum.

Bright lights and a crowd of press greeted a row of arriving limousines. From his distance, it looked like tiny figures stepping out of tiny Matchbox cars. Robin could just make out the black tuxedos on most of the men. The women must have been wearing colorful gowns. Spots of glittering blues and forest greens dotted the red carpet leading up to the museum entrance.

This was a big event. The gala of the year! And only the rich and famous had invitations.

Robin didn't usually pay attention to what the wealthy and powerful did for entertainment. He preferred a quiet night home alone, reading. Or skateboarding with his friends, especially now that they had the start of their own skatepark.

But Robin knew about the gala because of the FBI. They had the party on their radar. Unlike most events this spectacular, this shindig seemed to have been thrown together at the last minute. And at the last minute by the owner of the Museum of Arts and Culture. A certain Marlin Ledger.

The gala itself wasn't supposed to be eventful. That's why the FBI had "invited" Robin and his team to attend it. The real invitations came at the steep price tag of ten thousand dollars each.

Apparently, it was some sort of fundraiser. Something about helping the starving children in Opar. Which was interesting, since it was being put on by a man who had just lost a vast amount of money. Money that wasn't supposed to exist in the first place.

"Alright, you ready to do this?" Chad asked.

Robin nodded.

"Are you gonna do your thing again?" Chad mockingly waved his arms like he was falling.

"Probably not," Robin said coolly. "But who knows? Sometimes I like to play it a little risky."

"Uh-huh. Sure you do," Chad said, disappearing over the edge.

10

THE FBI COULDN'T EXACTLY stop the fundraising gala. For the time being, it was still a free country. Even would-be terrorists could throw a party if they wanted to.

Their real focus was elsewhere. The FBI had gotten wind of an event that was supposed to occur at the end of the gala. Apparently, there was a fundraiser inside the fundraiser.

An auction.

Only, no one had been able to determine what was being auctioned off.

Robin's shoes landed on the rooftop. It felt good to touch solid ground again. Robin might have leaned over and kissed it, if they didn't have work to do. And if Chad hadn't been watching.

"Houston," Robin's finger pressed on his earpiece. "Tranquility Base here. The Eagle has landed."

"Good to hear," Isabella responded. "And if we're going to continue using NASA metaphors, please make your way to the lunar lander. You have the green light."

"Roger that," Robin said, wrapping up a rope. "Oh, one more thing. How's that new software for the alarm system? What's your status on that?"

"Do you want me to use a lunar metaphor?"

"No, plain English will do."

"I have completed Project Alarm Mute, and it's now up and running."

"Good to hear." Robin hesitated. Was this a good time to fix the lie between them? Something felt off. But maybe he should wait to do that until they were face to face.

"Yes?" Isabella hesitated. "It sounded like you had more to say."

"Um, no, not really. But good job, Isabella. Over and out."

Finished packing up, Chad slung his backpack over one shoulder. He waited for Robin to coil the last length of rope.

"You know how we operate like a team, right?" Chad began pontificating. "And we get paid for it. So, that means we're like an official 'non-official' company, correct?"

"Chad, I'm not sure where you're going with this," Robin said, slipping on a pair of mirrored eyewear. With his backpack in order, Robin took the lead, tiptoeing over the rooftop.

"Okay. Let me cut to the chase. I think we should start writing our own business books. You know, a How to be Sneaky series."

Robin rolled his eyes. He slipped out his phone and studied the Google Maps satellite photos of the museum's rooftop. He changed their direction slightly.

"Listen, the way I see it, we're pretty much experts at what we do. You'd agree on that, right? Well, if we're a well-oiled business machine, then what we do could apply to other businesses. You know, to the day-to-day operations. You get it?"

Robin swung a leg up and over a large metal duct that crisscrossed the roof. With a bit of a hop, he slid over it. "You mean tripping booby traps and driving armored trucks while getting shot at?"

"Exactly!"

A drop in the roof approached. Maybe a six-foot drop. Robin spun around and lowered himself down. "I'm sorry. I fail to see how any of that translates into ordinary business."

Chad prepared to lower himself over the ledge, but then he paused. "Wait a minute. Is that supposed to be a joke?" His feet swung over the edge like an impatient child. "I can see about a thousand different connections!"

Robin looked back. "You *do* understand that you can't talk about what we do on the job, right?"

"Oh, of course," Chad chirped, hopping off his perch. "I'd use fake names. Aliases. Metaphors."

Robin pressed on, sidestepping an electrical conduit. "And you can't mention who we've investigated, or the locations of where we've been, or pretty much *anything* that could connect us to what we do, yes?"

"Sure, I don't have a problem with that."

"Wow. Then, yes. I think it would be an amazing business book, and you should most definitely write it."

"Are you serious?" Chad glowed.

"NO! I was lying," Robin growled. He went back to studying his phone. Nothing seemed to make sense. The satellite photos must have been old. "Ugh. How come GPS directions don't work up here?!"

"Hey, since you just shot down my brilliant book idea, what if I get into that?"

"That? What's *that*?"

"Software to help navigate rooftops, huh? There probably isn't much competition."

11

Isabella's chair creaked when she sat back in it. She had the rooftop vent open a crack. Everything was set.

Only . . . Project Alarm Mute wasn't 100% done. More like 95%. Maybe 90%.

She may have fudged things a little with Robin. Exaggerated a smidge. But she didn't want him to worry. He had enough to focus on, up on the roof.

All that mattered was that Isabella had completed the most important part of the code. The main alarm system inside the museum was now under her control. That was all that *really* mattered. Her teammates didn't need to know all the details.

Okay, Project Alarm Mute was maybe 85% complete. But Isabella would fix it. She had the time! In fact, pretty much all she had was time. This mission was destined to be a snoozer. It looked like another boring night of babysitting the computer systems and monitors. After all, the only thing the FBI wanted was information.

Isabella leaned forward and began typing again. She could finish the alarm code. With all the time she had on her hands, she'd hunt down the remaining bugs in the next half hour.

Okay, maybe an hour, max.

The FBI believed the mark was trying to sell a piece of artwork. A painting, or maybe a statue? What kind of art exactly wasn't known. Only that the mark needed to generate a lot of money, and fast.

Isabella typed in RUN, testing out the latest fixes to her program. ERROR (LINE 2472).

Hmm. What would cause that bug? She scrolled through page after page of C++ coding.

A boatload of money was going to exchange hands tonight. All the team had to do was get inside and document it.

Isabella sighed. Line 2472 of her code looked fine. No mistakes there. So, what wasn't working? There must be something going on under the surface causing the whole thing to error out.

A malfunction.

Isabella's chair creaked again as she leaned back.

Entry and documentation. Observation only.

Yeah, right. Like it was going to be *that* easy.

And like Robin could be content to "merely observe."

12

On top of the museum, Robin knelt before a large, boxy ventilation unit. He unscrewed the faceplate laboriously. There were countless screws holding the thing together. Robin's tiny handheld screwdriver groaned under the load.

Only inches away from his face, the fan blades inside the housing continued to spin. The blades were quick enough to create a blur.

When the last screw dropped to the gravel rooftop, Robin gingerly lifted the faceplate away. He rotated and set it down quietly on the rooftop.

Robin crouched before the blades, now fully exposed. Well-oiled, they were quiet. A silent killer if the next part went wrong.

Robin and Chad had practiced the art of stopping a fan blade all week. They even created a dummy fan to experiment with. A practice model with foam noodles and an old motor. Their test phase had gone relatively well. With all their practice, the boys knew exactly what they were doing. But now it was the real deal. And

Robin couldn't help remembering how many fingers they "lost" in practice. The blades were no longer pool noodles.

It gave Robin pause.

Of course, before Chad could take part, he simply "had" to do something first. He leaned in close to the fan. "Luke, I *am* your father."

Robin punched him.

Chad punched him back.

And Robin punched him one more time. "Can we be done now?"

"Yes, thank you. That would have bothered me all night if I didn't get it out of my system, you know? I probably would have yammered about it incessantly."

"You mean, like you're doing now?"

Chad nodded. "And I'm pretty sure nobody wants that. Because when I get stuck on one subject, I usually can go on and on. That's just part of my ADHD, you know?"

Robin tuned Chad out as they both slipped on their leather gloves again. Other tools were already spread out on the rooftop before them.

"I don't know if you know that about me, but I'm a talker. And if what my mother says is true, I seem to fixate on things." After cracking his neck side to side, Chad picked up a set of pliers. Opening the tool, he eased them toward the center of the spinning fan.

"I think talking helps to calm my nerves. Does that work for you the same way? 'Cause maybe that's just genetics, or maybe it's my meds. I don't know."

Like a surgeon, Chad pinched the pliers slowly, gingerly. As he gripped the central axle of the fan, it began to whine and groan.

Was the fan actually slowing down?

Yes. Robin could see the individual blades now. But it looked like they were still spinning fast. Faster than their practice setup.

"If my talking gets to be too much, you can just tell me. Honest. I can stop whenever you want me to—just in case you didn't think that was possible."

Robin took a deep breath. He didn't know if all that talking was helping or hurting. Helping Chad? Yes, probably. Helping Robin? No.

Robin grabbed the crowbar. Now it was his turn.

Bracing himself, Robin hunkered down like a football lineman ready for the snap of the ball. He could only hope that all their practice had prepared him. Should he limber up like Chad? Crack his neck? Did that really help or was it just stupid?

"You know, maybe if I start writing my own business books, I should get into recording audiobooks as well. I could be the narrator, don't you think? I mean, tell me if I'm wrong, but I do like to talk."

Robin said a silent prayer . . .

And then rammed the crowbar into the spinning blades!

TH-WHACKKK, WHACK, WHACK!

Robin felt the impact through his whole body. It was like hitting a baseball all wrong. The blow of metal on metal shot deep into Robin's bones.

But he had done it. The fan blades stopped.

Momentarily.

"Okay, stop talking now, will ya?" Robin grunted under the pressure. The force of the blade on his crowbar was immense. It took everything that Robin had to keep the fan still.

Chad leaned in. "Luke, I am no longer your father. Wow, that's weird how it doesn't work when the blades aren't—"

"Unscrew it, Chad! I'm not joking. Unscrew it NOW!" Robin yelled. He could feel the burn of lactic acid eating away at his muscles. "I . . . I don't know how long I can hold this!"

13

ANIKA SIMPLY HAD TO take a break.

She didn't care if she got fired. Actually, getting fired right now would be a mercy. Burning tears fully flowed down her cheeks. She'd be lucky to find her way to the restrooms.

Anika clawed at her apron, untying it. She yanked off her food prep hat. She wasn't exactly supposed to leave her station, but she didn't care. Anika grabbed an empty platter and held it above one shoulder.

She staggered her way past more busy employees and servers, all moving this way or that in a frenzy. With her eyes red and stinging like they were, she tried to keep her head down.

The smells drifting through the kitchen areas were wonderful. There were mountains of prime rib, roasted asparagus—even crème brûlée. Anika noted it all by smell. She had to remember to steer Chad clear of this area of the museum. That or the team would have one member go AWOL. Absent without leave!

Anika pushed through a set of double doors that easily swung open for her.

She paused. This was no longer the kitchen or workmen's area. Before Anika lay the Gallery of Impressionism.

Lifesize paintings adorned the walls. Mixes of blues and aquamarine greens were splashed about. Pinks and royal purples. What looked like simple dabs of paint worked in combination with each other as she stood back. Images emerged, taking shape. Stunning! Lifelike!

Rowboats set adrift on ponds.

Lily pads reflected in the water.

Dancers stretching at the barre.

With tears still streaking down her face, Anika couldn't stay here. Guests in their expensive finery milled about, taking in the art, chitchatting. She was completely out of place.

Anika spun around, ready to retreat, when a voice spoke to her.

"Excuse me. I'm done with this."

Anika turned back around. Had her supervisor found her?!

A lady stood before her, limply holding out an empty champagne flute. Her dress loudly announced its value, made from a deep hunter green silk with a long slit up the leg. A thin belt lay across her waist, glittering with jewels. Her dark brown hair hung down over one shoulder like a motionless river, each curl perfectly positioned. The lady continued her conversation with her tuxedo-wearing date, champagne flute now dangling from her fingertips.

"Um . . . yes, ma'am." Anika said, taking the glass. She looked around. Now where should she put it? And then she remembered her empty platter. Hello. That's right.

Anika set the glass on her tray as two more appetizer plates were added by others passing by.

Had no one noticed how out of place she was? Not even her red eyes and onion tears?

Anika grinned. She was practically invisible. She could go wherever she wanted and be completely ignored, overlooked.

Perfect!

14

"ARGH! You're killing me, Chad," Robin grunted, trying to renew his grip on the crowbar.

The torque on the fan was immense. It had to be significantly stronger than what they had practiced with.

"I'm going as fast as I can!" Chad hollered. He was reaching through the blades with both of his arms. All of Chad's work had to be done on the inside of the fan. "Stop putting me under so much pressure. You know that I can't handle a lot of pressure. I'm probably going to go slower if you keep yelling at me!"

"Okay . . . I'm sorry." Robin tried to say the words calmly. Act normal. But it was hard to hide the powerful force he was under. His back burned and ached. The thigh muscle in his left leg began twitching.

Chad continued to unscrew the blade assembly. Both his arms were deep inside the unit, threaded between the fan blades. But every time Chad unscrewed one hex nut, it only revealed another. "I don't understand. This fan isn't normal. We looked this up. Who makes a fan this complicated? I mean, really?!"

A high-pitched whine emanated from the motor, along with a thin ribbon of black smoke.

"Okay, just one more bolt—I can feel it!" Chad offered, smiling over his shoulder. Robin's face could no longer hide the pain. "At least, I think it's only one more bolt."

Robin could barely feel his arms. The pressure on the crowbar also pulled at his gloves. And sweating like he was sure wasn't helping. Robin had maybe another ten seconds. *Maybe.* Then his arms would give out. The engine would rip off his gloves, along with Chad's arms. "No, I can't do it. You have to pull your arms out, Chad."

"No, I'm almost done. I can feel it."

"Seriously, Chad. I'm trying my best to not stress you out!"

"One. More. Second!"

Tell him the truth.

Robin clamped his eyes shut. If only he had superhuman strength! "I can't—hold it—any longer!" Robin groaned as his legs buckled, dropping him to his knees. "I'M NOT STRONG ENOUGH!"

It happened so quickly.

Chad yanked himself backward—

Just as Robin's crowbar slipped.

CLANG-CLANG-CLAKKK!

Hot sparks splattered everywhere. The fan blades jumped back to life, spinning at a million miles per second. The force of the engine ripped the crowbar out of Robin's hands. Whistling through the air, the crowbar windmilled before coming to an abrupt stop—*KR-THUNK!*—twenty feet away, embedded deep into another ventilation shaft.

Yet that wasn't the worst of it.

A look of horror suddenly washed over Chad's face. He slowly held up one hand.

Two of his fingers were gone, severed through—

At least, until his hand slid fully back into the glove. All of his fingers wiggled like normal, unharmed, two of them sticking out from torn finger holes. The fan blades had only slashed the leather.

Both boys sighed.

"I'm sorry," Robin said, trying to rub his arms. He felt paralyzed and yet both his hands continued to shake. "I thought I could hold it, but that power . . . it was more than I could manage."

"No worries," Chad said, standing up and taking a step back. "You held it just long enough."

"What do you mean? It's still running . . ."

"Not for long." Chad took another step back.

Robin blinked. "Chad, we failed. *I* failed. We were supposed to stop the fan and—"

KR-TINKER, TINKER, TINK!

The fan clattered, making a terrible sound. It wobbled off-center.

"Robin," Chad motioned with his hand. "You might want to step away from the—"

Too late!

BLAMMM!

The spinning fan broke free, launching up . . . up . . . up into the air.

What now?! Robin took a step left. Then a step right. He didn't know the correct way to go. Instead, both boys hunkered down, covering their heads.

KR-THUNK!

The horrible fan blades, now twisted and bent, sunk into the rubbery rooftop exactly between Robin and Chad.

Silence.

While Robin stayed frozen, looking on in horror at what had nearly decapitated him, Chad stood and shrugged. He dusted himself off like nothing had just happened.

"I suppose it was good you didn't back up just then."

15

Anika slipped her tray of dirty dishes onto the bathroom counter.

Running the faucet, she hunched over, cupped the cool water in her hand, and rinsed out her eyes, over and over. It felt good. After a few more rinses, Anika looked up at herself in the mirror.

Red eyes. So much for that. They would only go away with time. As for her missing eyeliner, that could always be fixed. Later.

Anika reached up for a paper towel from the dispenser.

Empty.

She wandered over to another dispenser. That one was empty as well.

Great. Was she going to have to use her uniform to dry her face?

No. There was always toilet paper.

But as she slipped inside a stall, she heard heels enter the bathroom. One set? No, two. Anika quietly pulled the stall door closed. She didn't want the interruption, and she didn't feel like explaining why a member of the staff was using the regular restrooms.

"Good evening, Margarette," a silky voice said.

"Oh hello, Jenelle. I thought that might be you. How have you been?"

While the ladies chitchatted, Anika quietly unspooled a length of toilet paper. She used it to dab at her face. Anika had no interest in eavesdropping on other people's conversations. But then again, she was trapped.

"You wouldn't be here to do a little shopping, would you?"

"Oh, I don't know. I just might be. You?"

The two voices continued their conversation as Anika gently lowered the toilet lid.

"I suppose that depends on what's for sale. You wouldn't have any idea of what is up for auction, do you?"

"Margarette, I'm shocked," the second voice—Jenelle—said playfully. "You know we're not supposed to discuss this. At least not in public."

Anika quietly stepped up onto the toilet seat, just as one of the stall doors banged open. They were looking for her! Or rather, for anyone who might be listening in. Only, this information was exactly what Sneaky, Inc. had come for. What could Anika do?!

BANG . . . BANG . . . *BANG!*

A lady in a long azure gown made of taffeta silk pushed each stall door wide. Glancing inside until she was convinced that no one was hiding, the lady moved on. One after another, the doors shuddered open on their hinges.

Until she came to Anika's stall.

And when that last stall door flew open—

No one was there either.

But if the lady had looked upward, she would have seen something. A ceiling tile quietly slipping back into place.

"You can't be too careful, Margarette. I'd hate to be the one who is taken out back and shot. You know what they say: loose lips sink ships." The ladies laughed.

They had to be joking, right? And what was that about sinking ships? Did they really mean it, or was it just an old saying? Anika's muscles strained as she stretched out spiderlike on top of the thin ceiling rafters. Any movement would likely make a noise. Anika remained frozen in place.

The women's voices got quieter, but Anika could just make out the words.

"I've heard that this is a once-in-a-lifetime opportunity. Something that has surfaced after years of being hidden away. Even the black market is all abuzz and quite interested."

"Yes, that's what I've heard also. But do you have any insider information on *what* it is? What it could be?"

Anika's leg suddenly slipped.

TINK.

Her foot hit a ceiling tile. Not too loud, but enough to be heard.

There was silence below.

Anika held her breath. Did she spook the ladies? Had they left? Anika would have heard the bathroom door, right? Maybe they had begun searching the bathroom again.

No. The voices came again, now almost imperceptible. Little more than whispers.

Anika could barely hear anything. Did she dare wriggle forward? Just a little closer?

"I don't know exactly," came Jenelle's voice. "But if my hunches are correct, it might just be *a girl's best friend*."

16

Isabella sat up straighter.

The computer code *still* wasn't making any sense. Go figure. And now, in trying to fix one thing, she had broken another.

Her fingers drummed against her lower lip. Why wasn't this working correctly?

Command + Z = Undo.

Isabella pressed the key combination several times, erasing everything new that she had just done.

What was happening to her? Had she forgotten how basic coding worked?

No, this was just complicated. Complicated on purpose! The museum security didn't want anyone hacking into their code. They probably had spent millions on this custom system. No wonder it wasn't easy to hack.

Isabella simply needed to chill out. Put on some tunes. Do something to calm her nerves.

On the computer screen, Isabella pulled up another window.

The splash screen displayed the word Minecraft.

Digging through the settings, Isabella set the game to "peaceful." That way, she wouldn't hear any of the zombie or skeleton noises.

Gentle music began drifting out of the trailer's mounted speakers, creating the perfect surround sound. Isabella simply loved the soundtrack. It reminded her of when she was young. Of the long summer days without school. She thought back on fireflies blinking outside the window screen while she played late into the night. Back when life was somehow easier.

Back when her dad was still around.

Before everything changed.

17

Robin and Chad slid down through the ventilation shafts. They were inside the museum now. It wasn't difficult making progress with gravity helping to pull them along.

But then their momentum stopped—the shafts leveled out.

Robin cracked a glow stick and shook it. The pale yellow light steadily grew.

He took the moment to massage his arm muscles. They still ached from the work with the crowbar. From holding back the powerful drive of the fan blades. Why was that so similar to what it felt like to hold a lie? Heavy. Growing ever heavier.

Robin pushed the thoughts out of his head. He had work to do. And this was quickly becoming a stupid conversation in his mind.

Only somehow it felt true.

But it wasn't a big lie! It was small and worth forgetting about. So why couldn't he?!

Robin offered up a silent prayer. "Dear Jesus, please forgive me for lying to Isabella. Amen." He held up the glow stick to get a better view of their path ahead. "Oh, and for the life of me, can you please stop letting it come to mind? Thanks."

A rectangle of darkness lay ahead.

A tiny metal room opened up before Robin and Chad. A ventilation junction box.

Robin strained his neck, bending his head to fit inside. That, or he needed to squat and wobble forward like an ape. Neither option felt great.

On the other hand, Chad fit perfectly. His hair brushed against the ceiling, but otherwise he moved about like normal.

Both boys fished through their backpacks. While Robin pulled out a cordless drill and a towel, Chad withdrew a repelling pulley. Robin wrapped the drill in the thick towel. Holding it up next to his face, he began screwing a bolt into the ceiling of the junction box.

Chad threaded a rappel line through his harness and into the pulley.

With Robin's drilling complete, Chad clipped the pulley onto the ceiling bolt. Robin tucked away the drill and produced a suction cup on a long ball of string.

Chad slipped on a pair of dark goggles and began striking the top of what looked like a road flare.

"Give me a second before you light that thing," Robin whispered.

Bending over, Robin licked the suction cup and pressed it firmly onto the center of their cramped patch of floor. Then, holding onto the string, Robin leaned back, closing his eyes and shielding his face, and nodded to Chad.

Chad struck the road flare again.

A blinding light ignited, turning their dimly-lit box bright as daylight.

Chad used the vapor metal torch to cut out a ring in the floor. And just as quickly, he used the cap to snuff out the flame.

Robin opened his eyes. Despite having kept them tightly closed, he still saw spots.

Hand over hand, Robin lowered the string attached to the suction cup. The circular piece of metal flooring lowered into the dim room below. Further . . . further . . . until—

KR-TINK!

The string went slack. The metal must have reached the floor below. Robin let the rest of the string go. He watched it snake through his hands and disappear into the darkness.

Chad clipped in. Holding one end of the rope behind himself, he slowly lowered himself through the opening.

Robin waited his turn.

Except he didn't like waiting. There was nothing good to do while waiting. Especially when it involved heights again. Okay, yes, he could pray. He thought about doing that some more. But he didn't exactly have anything else to pray about.

And he didn't want the former topic to return.

Where was Chad? Wasn't he down already?!

The rope suddenly jerked twice. That was their signal.

Robin threaded the rope through his harness. Holding it snugly against his lower back, Robin stepped out into thin air.

"Lord, help me!" he whispered through clenched teeth.

Okay, so maybe there was something left to pray about.

Everything held. Just like it was supposed to. The rappelling rope caught and tightened. Robin never liked that first step. He squeezed the rope tighter trying to stop his hands from shaking.

The first step always felt like falling.

Robin let out more rope. He descended steadily into a vast room of the museum. Through the haze of darkness, he could just make out human figures. All in various poses, frozen in time.

Lifelike statues carved out of marble continued to materialize into view. Some were ancient figures in the middle of a great battle, or timid water-carriers lifting their daily collection. One statue depicted a fallen figure sheltered in the arms of their lover.

Robin lowered himself further.

The room was eerily quiet and cold. This was a place used to crowds of visitors, international guests, and schoolchildren on field trips. To witness it as such a dim and lifeless setting unnerved Robin.

It felt wrong to be there.

And where was Chad?! He hadn't gone on ahead without Robin, had he?

Robin's feet softly touched the ground. His rappel line went slack. Robin glanced around. No sign of his partner. No sign of his friend.

Robin yanked on one side of the rope, pulling it free from the pulley above. Stepping aside, Robin watched the rope silently fall, snaking into a puddle on the floor.

Had something just moved?

Over there, to his side?

Robin slipped out a penlight. He hesitated. Was it worth turning it on?

No. It was all in his imagination. Robin coiled up the rope. It was too incriminating to leave behind. Over his elbow and through his hand, he continued to wrap it. Pausing only for a moment.

Long enough to look around again.

Did he dare call out for Chad? Even a whisper? His mouth was unusually dry.

It almost felt like the statues were moving closer.

Like they were alive.

Suddenly, there was a groan—and one of the dying figures stumbled to its feet!

18

WITH ITS ARMS OUTSTRETCHED, the statue ambled closer.

Within a foot of Robin, the figure flicked on a flashlight and held it just under its chin. The light cast an unnatural glow over its face.

"I vant to suck your blood," Chad growled.

Robin continued winding the rope like nothing happened. Pretended his heart wasn't hammering. Securing the end of the line, Robin shoved the entire coil into Chad's chest. "Here, make yourself useful."

"But what did you think? Wasn't that at least kinda spooky?"

Robin pulled out his phone and studied the visitor's map. "No."

"Oh, I *bet* I had your ticker beating a little faster. I know that was kind of a mix of monsters I had going there. I was walking like a mummy, but then I talked like a vampire. Did that lose it for ya?"

Robin didn't answer. Instead, he oriented himself to the map and headed west.

Chad shoved the rope into his backpack and raced to keep up.

"I wonder if we could rent out the museum for a Halloween party. You could make a pretty good haunted house through that room, yes?"

Robin slipped into a new room.

Pottery and vases in various states of decay stood on platforms. Stanchions quarantined them off with red velvet ropes, barring any approach. Scenes of ancient Greek life wrapped across the pottery. Flat characters going about their flat lives. They almost looked like the doodles Robin would make in the margins of his notepaper at school. Only these drawings were priceless.

"Ever wonder what makes all this stuff so valuable?" Chad mused. He paused to stare at a piece that was decorated to look like an octopus.

"Not really."

"I mean, do you think two thousand years from now, if someone found a pair of my underwear, it might show up here? In a museum?"

"It's possible."

"How so?"

"It's possible because of the rate you change—or rather *don't* change—your underwear. There's a good chance they'd be completely petrified by then. So, yes. They will easily survive and will probably be on display here two millennia from now."

Chad actually looked like he was weighing the idea. "That. Would. Be. Cool."

Gallery after gallery, the boys slipped forward, weaving their way through the dark side of the museum. They carefully steered away from anything to do with the gala. The distant noises of festive music and voices never rose above a low rumble. Like listening to a pool party from below the surface of the water.

There were very few guards here. And with the ones that were there, Robin and Chad took the long way around them.

But it was somewhere in the eighteenth-century room that things got dicey.

Elaborate costumes from the days of King George III were on display. Headless mannequins wore gold filigree, tall collars, and layers upon layers of heavy cloth. It all looked hot and uncomfortable.

Chad noticed it first.

A shadow across the floor.

It had moved.

A guard? A guest? It didn't matter.

Someone was up ahead.

And since this was the only route forward, Robin and Chad had to proceed.

Using hand signals, the boys split up. The hope was to circle around the individual, flank him or her. If they could, they would remain invisible and move on. But they knew that their luck might run out at some point.

Robin inched forward.

This was no big deal. The guards weren't expecting anyone to come from the inside. They were too busy keeping the curious party guests *out*.

Up ahead, Robin spied something that looked out of place. Something sitting on the floor.

It almost looked like a backpack.

Or maybe a large purse?

Robin hesitated. Should he move closer? Or maybe now was the time to stay clear of it.

Too risky, he decided. It was too dark to see what was on the floor. He'd practically have to get right up to the object before he could make it out. Instead, Robin doubled back.

And that's when someone hit him—

From behind!

19

A GIRL'S BEST FRIEND. Was that supposed to be a clue? It didn't make any sense to Anika.

She slipped off her backpack. She didn't want the weight of it slowing her down.

Besides, maybe it would distract the guard who was sneaking up behind her.

Anika slipped into the shadows.

She didn't like the idea of hitting someone over the head, but it came with the job.

Sure enough, there he was. A silhouette in the faint light. She watched as the guard inched forward, trying to get the better of her. He moved closer to her backpack.

Clinging to the outer edges of the room, Anika doubled back and slipped behind the figure.

She raised her blackjack. It was a short, leather club, useful in a pinch. Then again, Anika had never actually had to use it yet. It seemed so crude, but it was one of the few weapons that didn't kill. It would only incapacitate.

Before she swung the club, Anika had a faint sense of recognition. The figure in front of her seemed familiar. Something about the outline?

But that didn't stop her.

When Robin came to, he found himself looking up at Anika from an odd angle. She was cradling his head in her lap. Very odd.

And the headache he now had was like—WOW! It throbbed as though someone had hit him over the head.

Wait a minute. It was all coming back to him. Just as Anika whispered, "I'm so, *so* sorry, Robin. I couldn't tell that it was you in the dark. Honest! I would never have hit you if I had known who you were."

Someone beside them snickered.

Chad!

Reaching for the back of his head, Robin tried to sit up. The floor began to move. It tilted to one side. Then it tilted in the other direction.

"We have to . . ." Robin tried standing. Was he on a boat, far out at sea? "We have to keep going."

Off balance, Robin bumped into a glass display case, setting it rattling. But Chad's quick hands grabbed it, preventing it from falling.

"Maybe you should rest a little more," Anika whispered, putting her hands on Robin's shoulders. "We still have time before the auction. And all we have to do is document the item up for sale. A few photographs, then we're done."

"Thank goodness the Men in Black don't need us to haul out some gigantic oil landscape or something," Chad remarked. "Although I did see a statue back there that I wouldn't mind having in my bedroom. It probably weighs a ton. But you know, if we all lifted at exactly the same time—"

Robin staggered forward, pulling out his phone. "But the FBI wants us to document it. We have to photograph it." Robin couldn't understand why his phone wouldn't turn on.

"Hello? That's what she just said."

Oh, he was swiping up the *back* of his phone. "Maybe I should rest a little more," Robin said, slipping back down into a seated position.

"Man, did Anika knock something loose in there, huh?"

20

AFTER TWO ASPIRIN AND a lot of staring up at the water sprinkler until the ceiling tiles stopped moving, Robin felt a little better. At least enough to walk.

The FBI predicted the auction would take place in the Great Hall. It was one of the few rooms in the museum that could handle a larger crowd.

Clinging to the shadows, Robin and his team approached the third-floor balcony. Peering down, it was easy to see that only the first floor was still lit and open to the gala.

The Great Hall was nothing short of its namesake. Fully illuminated, the polished marble floor spilled out over the size of several football fields. The hall housed the museum's temporary displays. A visiting exhibit from Egypt currently occupied the space, featuring stone obelisks, ornate headdresses from the pharaohs, and even the sarcophagus of a mummy.

Along one of the walls, the museum had installed a five-hundred-thousand-gallon fish tank. A cylindrical behemoth towering three stories tall, it sported an entire ecosystem of colorful fish.

But what made the Great Hall even more spectacular were the aircraft hanging from the rafters.

A replica of Orville and Wilbur Wright's aircraft dangled above. Several fighter aircraft from both World Wars also hung there, along with other lesser-known aircraft.

But the most magnificent piece was a B-29 Superfortress. At ninety-nine feet long, the World War II relic was suspended at center stage. Its entire body, skinned with shiny metal and thousands of rivets, reflected its surroundings. Windows encircled the nose cone and rear gunner's seat. And standing nearly as tall as two-story houses, two sixteen-foot-wide propellers protruded from each of the wings.

The museum building was a true feat of engineering. The ceiling had to be holding hundreds of thousands of pounds. There were so many aircraft above the guests' heads that the planes nearly touched wing to wing.

Robin retrieved a pair of digital binoculars from his backpack and surveyed the ground level.

It wasn't difficult to find the area of everyone's focus. Marlin Ledger had spared no expense to build and design this area. Gold torches blazed with real fire in elaborately carved stands. Spotlights all trained the attention to one location.

Half a dozen guards surrounded the illuminated exhibit. Were they merely for show? To drive up the bidding cost and the impression of how much the object was worth?

CLICK, CLICK. Robin zoomed in further.

German G3 automatic rifles. They looked real enough. Likely the guards were more goons from Ledger's kill squad.

Robin trained the binoculars on what the guards had surrounded.

A solitary exhibit stood at the center. Small compared to the spectacles that surrounded it.

A pure-white pedestal held the prize.

Instead of something large and grandiose, as Robin had expected, the item was small and compact. Nestled in the center of a deep blue satin pillow trimmed in gold sat—

A diamond.

It was almost the size of a golf ball, cut beautifully and shimmering in the lights.

Robin pulled the binoculars momentarily away from his eyes. He fiddled with the settings on top, activating a live video stream back to Isabella.

CLICK, CLICK. He zoomed in even further.

This was no ordinary treasure. If its size wasn't remarkable enough, the jewel looked almost like it glowed from within. The center of the diamond glimmered with brightly colored streaks of reds and oranges. Almost as if the diamond had tongues of fire flickering within it!

L'Étoile de Flamme Diamant.

At least, that's what the sign read.

Robin pressed his earpiece. "Are you getting this, Isabella?"

"Oh, I'm getting it alright. I wouldn't mind having one of those. Think I can order one off of Amazon?"

"Ha! Yeah right."

"I just Googled those words," Isabella continued quietly. "It's French. It literally translates as the Star of Flame Diamond." Isabella went silent. "Hmm, interesting."

"Interesting?" Anika asked. "How so?"

"I'm skimming the Wikipedia page. It says that the Star of Flame Diamond was once owned by a Russian dynasty. A monarch named Catherine the Great, apparently. Oh—and get this. It has an 'inestimable value' since historians presumed it was lost for good. Blah, blah . . . wow! You're not going to believe this! It's been missing ever since the Battle of Paris . . . in 1814!"

21

"THIS CHANGES EVERYTHING," ROBIN whispered. He crept back into the darkness of the nearby gallery. Fiddling with the binoculars, he slipped out the micro SD chip and snapped it into a little case for safekeeping.

"Changes what?" Chad slid back beside him. "What does it change?"

"I know what you're thinking, Robin," Anika said, shaking her head disapprovingly. "But we need to stick to our orders. We have the photos that we came for. We have the evidence. The FBI hasn't given us the green light to do anything more."

But Robin wasn't listening. He stood up, pacing. His aching head tilted back, pointed up at the ceiling. "You do understand why our mark is after the money, right? Why he would pull something like this out of hiding? After it's been hidden for centuries!"

Chad cleared his throat. "Yeah, because we took his play money."

"Robin, we saw one piece of paper in his office," Anika said, rather coldly. "One sheet that hinted at a so-called master plan to target

Washington, DC. If it's really all that horrible, then why hasn't the FBI swooped in and arrested him? We don't know for certain that's what our mark plans to do with the money. What if he's using it to somehow try to *stop* the terrorists?"

Robin leaned in close, his voice little more than a whisper. "That paper mentioned a nuclear weapon. Do you have any idea how powerful they are now? Forget what you learned about World War II. First, Washington, DC, will disappear. Vaporized in the blink of an eye with nothing left other than ash and smoke. But it doesn't stop there. The concussion from the explosion will spread out, leveling Baltimore, Philadelphia, even Richmond. And then there's the fallout—a wildfire eating everything in its path. An invisible poison that will engulf everything east of the Mississippi."

That brought a silence over the group.

Robin's fingers drummed on the side of his pant leg. "I bet it wouldn't be hard to swipe, you know."

"Oh, really?" Anika said, rolling her eyes. "One of us will just walk down there and toss the diamond in their pocket?"

"Just think about all this for a moment. Our mark is charging an arm and a leg for the elite just to get into this party, right? Then, as if that wasn't enough money, our mark somehow gets his hands on a long-lost diamond. Maybe he finds it on the black market. Or maybe he's been sitting on it for years, who knows. But now he's ready to sell it. A quick grab for cash. If he does sell it, how much money will that give him, huh? We'll never get back into his vaults. I'm sure he's completely changed all of his security codes and procedures and moved everything around. The FBI will never have enough time to work up the intel on his new hiding spot for that much money. If we don't grab the diamond now, while it's still small enough to fit in one of our pockets . . . then we *never* will. And he'll be able to do whatever he wants with the money."

"I'm in," Chad said, eagerly raising his hand.

"You don't have to raise your hand. We're not in school," Robin said. "Isabella, what do you think?"

Isabella's voice crackled from their earpieces. "I've got the easy job, sitting outside with hot chocolate and show tunes. It's not my neck on the line—not like it is yours. So I don't know how much my vote really counts. After all, if this Mr. Smith is really as bad as you say he is—"

Chad mouthed the words "Mr. Smith," clearly confused. Robin downplayed it by shaking his head.

"It's you guys who are in the hot seat," Isabella finished.

"Okay, we'll discuss it among ourselves and get back to you," Robin said. The three of them pressed their earpieces, shutting off communication with Isabella.

"Why did you tell her his name is Mr. Smith? You lied to her?"

"Because, Chad. It's on a need-to-know basis. And she doesn't need to know, alright? Can I be the leader of the group and not have everything I do constantly questioned?!"

Chad stepped back, clearly surprised at having touched on a sore spot.

Robin leaned in to Anika and whispered, "I need you in on this. There is no way we could do it without you."

"I don't have a good feeling about this, Robin." Anika shook her head. "I don't think we're ready for it. We haven't done any reconnaissance. We haven't studied up on the security surrounding the diamond itself. And for all I know, we don't even have a plan."

"I know. I agree with you on every point," Robin said. "But I *do* have a plan. Well, at least the start of a plan, if that helps. What else do you think we should do? Just take our photos and walk away?"

"Yeah. Why not, Robin? Why not just walk away for once? What's so wrong with that?!"

"You're right, you're right."

"Haven't we done enough? Haven't we done all that we've been asked?"

Robin nodded.

"One of these days, Robin, a job is going to blow up in our faces. And then what? Oops, oh well? Sorry?"

Robin felt the back of his head. A lump was growing where Anika had hit him. It hurt when he touched it. "I can't argue with you. You decide. I'll go along with your decision, alright?"

"Oh, great. So now the fate of the world is resting on my shoulders, is it?"

"No, no. The entire eastern seaboard maybe, but not the entire world," Robin said with a wry grin.

"Gee, somehow that doesn't make me feel any better," Anika said, pausing. "Alright. Let's do this."

22

"ALRIGHT, LISTEN UP," ROBIN said after pressing his earpiece again. "It's a go. If worst comes to worst, we'll bail and pull the plug—but we've got to give it a try. Now, we've already proven that we can work as a team, and I'd like to see that again. So, our number one issue is that we have to communicate with each other, got that? If any of us needs something, then we better speak up. We don't need any heroes today. So, please be real with each other—and most of all, be honest."

And when will you *be honest?*

It was a whisper, but it sounded loud and clear to Robin. Had anyone else heard that? Robin swallowed and hesitated before saying more. A cold drop of sweat ran down the side of his face. He wiped it away.

"Isabella, I want you to research this flame star thing."

"The Star of Flame Diamond."

"Yes." Robin hunched over and rearranged the items in his backpack. "I want you to find out anything and everything you can about it. And what are the chances you can make me a duplicate of it?"

"A copy of the diamond?" Isabella asked. "Oh, I don't know. Let me look into that."

Robin turned, looking for Chad. Wait, where *was* Chad?

Over at a nearby display of abstract paintings, Robin's friend had actually pulled one frame off the wall. Chad now held it in his hands.

"What are you doing?!" Robin hissed.

"Don't worry. Izzy's got the alarms off," Chad said over his shoulder. "Have you ever wondered how anyone knows which end is up with these paintings?" He rotated the abstract artwork ninety degrees. And then he rotated it again.

Robin's mouth hung open. To his surprise, the painting might have actually looked better on its side. Or was it now upside down? Or right side up?

It didn't matter! "Will you stop that?! That's a priceless piece of artwork you're messing with."

"Fine, okay," Chad said, rehanging the work. "Although I probably could have painted something better than this, don't you think?"

"Chad, your assignment is to get Anika's pack. Her duffel bag is back in the kitchen."

"Her pack, seriously? Why me? Why doesn't Anika get her own bag?"

"Because I need her to come with me."

"Alright, boss," Chad said, slipping off into the darkness.

"And keep your hands off the artwork!" Robin whisper-shouted after Chad. Did he hear Robin? It didn't matter. Chad was going to do whatever Chad wanted to do.

"And where are we going, boss?" Anika said with a smile.

"Don't—don't call me boss."

"How come Chad gets to call you that?"

"Because Chad is, well . . . Chad." Robin slung his backpack over a shoulder. "There's too much security to take that diamond straight on. And it's too open and exposed from above. We've got to find another way to approach it."

"Like finding a way to the underside of that diamond?"

"Exactly!"

23

Isabella pulled up Robin's photos of the Star of Flame Diamond.

She leaned in close, looking at it. Golly, wouldn't it be nice to own one of those? Maybe wear that to the next school dance?

Isabella Googled "diamond" and pulled up different images of the glittering stones on every monitor. She needed all the reference images she could find.

She clicked on a desktop icon.

In a moment, the splash screen read: Blender 3D.

Isabella clicked the splash screen away and deleted the default cube. How exactly did you model a diamond? There were so many facets to the shape . . . and so little time to add them. She chose a cone primitive and switched to edit mode. With "You'll be Back" from the *Hamilton* soundtrack playing in the background, Isabella began adding new vertices, pushing and pulling them as she went.

Using her other hand, Isabella slid her phone closer, holding the side button.

"Hey, Siri, find someone near me who offers 3D printing services."

I've found three businesses from the web.

"Hey, Siri, call the first business."

Isabella's phone dialed the number, beeped a few times, then got the voicemail. Isabella hung up.

"Hey, Siri, call the second business."

The phone dialed again. But then it played three robotic notes and a different recording played.

We're sorry. The number that you have dialed has been disconnected. If you feel—

Isabella smashed the red button, hanging up. This wasn't looking good. She only had one more option. Isabella glanced up at the clock. 9:36 p.m. Who was going to be open at this hour?!

"Hey, Siri, call the last business."

The phone dialed the number and it rang. Isabella spun her diamond model. It was no work of art, but it also wasn't half bad. Especially considering the software was open source and she hadn't used her modeling skills in months.

The phone continued to ring.

Isabella hit F12 and watched as the cycle's engine slowly rendered the complicated glass caustics.

"Hello?" a voice suddenly said. A male voice, groggy and rough. It sounded like he had just woken up.

"Oh, I'm sorry," Isabella said. "I must have the wrong number."

"Wait. Who were you trying to reach?"

Isabella swiped up on her phone, looking for the business name. "Um, Brad's Amazing Ender of the World Printing Service?" Was that really the name of the company? Isabella immediately felt embarrassed reading it out loud. Like ordering a goofy sandwich called Bob's Big Burger or the Fatburger with Bacon.

"Yeah, I'm Brad. Whatcha want?" he yawned.

"Um, this might be an autocorrect mistake, but do you actually offer 3D printing services?"

"Yeah. Look, I don't have some fancy business address, alright? Do you know what rent costs these days? I work out of my parents' house. You got something you need printed, I can print it."

Isabella couldn't believe her luck. Here was a business open at night. Okay, maybe business was a loose term, but at least some guy (who was probably scratching his belly right now) awake and willing to do the team's 3D printing!

"Can you do glass printing?"

"I've got a crystal-clear PLA. That's gonna cost you extra, just so you know."

"Oh, that's no problem. Can I send you the OBJ file?"

"Sure. When do you need it?"

Isabella cringed. "Um, in the next half hour?"

"Half an hour?!" There was silence. Was Brad climbing out of bed? "I'm going to have to lower the infill to get it out that fast. And that's definitely going to qualify as a rush job, which means—" There were some sounds of rustling papers. Was he looking up his pricing sheet?

Then it sounded like something fell.

He swore. "Sorry about that. I just bumped my Mega-Gulp Mountain Dew." It sounded like more things were falling. He swore again.

One of Isabella's eyebrows rose. *Give him grace, give him grace.* Was this what Robin had been talking about? It sounded like Brad could use all the second chances he could get.

"Yeah, well," Brad grunted. "A rush job is going to cost you more! A lot more!"

CRASH! Something else must have fallen. The voice suddenly got very calm and controlled. Like he was simply trying to hold it all together. Brad spoke through his teeth.

"How's a hundred and fifty bucks? That work?"

"Um, a hundred and fifty dollars?" Isabella said, rummaging through the team's cashbox. It was hard to tell how much was inside without properly counting it. But with what she had in her pocket too, it was probably enough. "Yup, that works."

"You gonna pick it up?"

Isabella quickly Googled the "company" address listed. It was on the other side of the city. "No, I'm sorry. I'm at work. Can we meet somewhere?" Isabella spun around in her seat. She glanced out of the trailer's tinted door window. "How about the Starbucks at Ridgemont and Third?"

"Seriously? You want me to deliver it?!"

"Yes?" Isabella cringed again. "Pretty please?" She bit her lip. Isabella hoped that maybe if she sounded like the classic damsel in distress, it would trigger this guy's more noble character.

If he had one.

Silence.

"Yeah, fine!" He didn't sound happy.

Isabella mouthed the next words at the same time Brad said them.

"But it'll cost you more!"

24

CHAD SKIPPED DOWN THE back staircase. His surroundings lay mostly in a gray light. The heavy marble walls and stairs felt gothic and oppressive.

Only, Chad thought about none of that. All he could think about at that moment was one thing.

A Super Ball!

It had to be one of the most underrated toys of all times. If Chad had a Super Ball right then, he would have thrown it. Man, he would have thrown that ball as hard as he could. Chad looked around him, trying to imagine just how many times it would have to bounce before it could come to a stop. It would probably bounce for days!

Chad ran a few numbers in his head. His estimate of Super Ball bounces was in the millions. But then again, Chad wasn't very good at statistics. For that matter, he wasn't very good at math.

Other than homeroom, Chad didn't really have a subject at school that he was very good at.

At least, not when he forgot to take his Focalin. His ADHD med. Like this morning, for example. He had the pill bottle open, and the orange juice poured and everything, when—

Chad paused, stopping on the museum steps.

Something had caught his attention. Chad was near an exhibit of headless mannequins displaying various suits of ancient samurai armor. He slipped out his phone.

Holding it up for a selfie, Chad tried to position his head above the mannequin.

Only he was a bit too short.

Chad inched up on his tippy-toes. Rats! He was still too short.

Why did God have to make him like this?! He asked Pastor Peter that once. Pastor Peter was his youth pastor at church. Chad got some lame answer about being made wonderfully. All stuff that youth pastors had to say.

Chad looked around. This photo was too good to pass up on. There had to be a chair around somewhere.

This *was* a museum, after all!

And Chad found a chair.

The little card said something about it being the chair of King Richard IV. Chad hadn't heard of the guy, so that felt like permission.

He dragged it from three exhibits away. Somehow Chad didn't remember it being that far away when he went looking for it.

Trying to be quiet, Chad pushed the lousy chair into position behind the samurai. Should he take off his shoes? Nah. One photo and he'd be done. Chad climbed up onto the antique. The chair had a nasty wobble to it. And it squeaked.

Chad held out his phone for a shot of his head positioned on top of a wicked-cool set of samurai armor. For what was surely going to be the coolest selfie of the century—or was it the decade? Wait, which one is longer?

A guard entered the gallery.

25

THE ENTRANCE TO THE basement was not easy to find.

Robin and Anika had to try *way* too many doors until they found it. It just wasn't the kind of location they labeled on the visitor's map.

And it took two sets of Anika's now-bent lockpicks to get inside.

Robin was regretting not bringing Chad along. Out of the entire Sneaky, Inc. team, Mr. Sticky was the best at lockpicking. A true natural. For Robin, it took lots of wiggling the picks around in no particular pattern. Even then, it was a 50/50 chance of unlocking anything at all.

Anika had more luck using her hand drill.

Anyway, it didn't matter now. They were in and heading down.

Robin and Anika couldn't talk much. There were guards down in the basement. At least, there were three of them in an underground guard shack they had to sneak past.

It gave Robin peace of mind that Isabella had successfully shut down the alarm system. To the museum's security team, everything showed green lights. Even if you happened to pass through a hidden laser, you were good to go.

The basement was simply huge. Nearly as big as the upstairs galleries.

It was less pretty, though. Concrete walls. Poor lighting. This was a vast underground storage area. But what surprised Robin was just how much artwork was down in the basement. There had to be just as much in storage as there was on display throughout the three floors above them.

One section looked like a warehouse, with thirty-foot-tall shelves. Crates of different sizes gathered dust, stacked floor to ceiling.

At least one room was vast enough to park several tractor trailers inside. There were loading/unloading ramps and a long incline for them to drive into the back of the museum.

Only, as Robin and Anika snuck forward, clinging to the shadows, they watched as two large trucks drove out of the museum. And just as quickly—

BEEP, BEEP, BEEP.

Two more trucks backed in.

The basement had been pretty quiet so far, but now there was quite a commotion ahead: a gathering of workers ready to meet the new trucks. Most of them wore full-length overalls and gloves. Were they part of the museum staff?

As soon as the vehicles came to a stop, the workers got busy.

Once the back of the truck rolled open, workers pushed crate after crate into the empty trailer. It was like watching a game of Tetris being played in real time.

With at least two dozen workers, the work went fast and efficiently.

It wasn't long before the first truck was full and pulled away from the dock, exiting the museum.

The same work began all over again with the second truck.

Why was so much loading work being done? And why at night? Wasn't that expensive, paying workers overtime?

Robin slowly lifted a device above his hiding spot. Using his digital binoculars, he spied the area ahead. A long line of crates varying in size were positioned behind the trucks. Were all of these awaiting departure?

Robin lowered the binoculars. He showed Anika the video playback on the tiny screen.

"I want to get a closer look at what's in those crates," Robin whispered.

Anika nodded.

26

INSIDE THE STARBUCKS, ISABELLA glanced at her phone's lock screen, reading the time. Brad was late.

Isabella had ordered a mocha and asked for double whipped cream. She needed it. Somehow the idea was that the creamy, sugary goodness would take away all her nervousness.

It didn't, but it still tasted good.

She took another sip, wiping away the cream from the tip of her nose. Would she even know this Brad when he walked into the shop? He couldn't be there already, could he? Waiting for her?

Isabella felt her throat tighten. From her seat, she scanned the surrounding patrons.

There was the guy in a tweed jacket. His hair was thinning, turning gray at the edges. He sat with a pretty lady who somehow looked like Rosie the Riveter, from the old World War II poster. Oh, it had to be the red bandana she wore in her hair. Both of them seemed more interested in their phones than in each other. The guy didn't look like a Brad.

Another man sat by himself. That could be Brad. He was reading from an issue of *Gardening* magazine.

The others in the coffee shop were all women. And one older gentleman who used a cane. He simply didn't strike Isabella as a guy who offered 3D printing services.

Did she dare approach the gardening reader? What would she say? "Hey, you got the goods? 'Cause I've got the money!" No, that sounded terrible.

She could just say, "Hey, I'm Isabella. Are you Brad?"

What if the guy's name just happened to be Brad too?!

Isabella sat back. She willed herself to relax. She took another swig. Hot. Too hot!

This meeting didn't have to be so difficult. It's not like she had ordered a hit on somebody and was now going to have coffee with the assassin.

It was a stupid lump of glass, that's all!

DING!

A little bell announced the side door opening. In shuffled a new person.

Isabella couldn't help but smile to herself.

The "gentleman"—if you could call him that—looked to be in his mid- to late twenties. He wore an ash gray T-shirt at least two sizes too small. The front read: PROGRAMMING: TURNING PIZZA AND COFFEE INTO CODE. His hair looked greasy, and he didn't look like he had shaved more recently than maybe a week ago.

Could this guy be any more stereotypical?

The guy sweated as he clutched a small brown paper bag closely in front of him. He didn't approach the counter. Instead, he scouted around those who were already seated.

For one brief second, their eyes met.

But the guy continued his search. His shoulders slouched. Was that disappointment?

Didn't Brad see her? Hello?! She hadn't given Brad any description of herself, but wasn't it obvious? She *was* the only female sitting alone.

And just as quickly, the guy spun on his heels, heading for the door.

Isabella waved her hand. She didn't want to draw attention, but she was about to lose this guy.

"BRAD!" She said his name louder than she wanted. It felt like the entire coffee shop stopped and turned to stare at her.

But so did the guy at the door.

Quickly enough, everyone turned back to their own conversations. The guy reluctantly approached Isabella. Hold on. Did she still have whipped cream on her face? Why was he so disgusted with her?

"*You're* Isabella?"

She nodded. Why didn't she use a fake name? Never use your real name! She knew that. Especially when she was on an operation! Isabella breathed in. She needed to give herself grace.

"You must be Brad," she said, pointing to the empty seat across from her.

"I don't believe this," Brad said with disdain. "You didn't tell me you were just a kid!" He winced at his own volume. Embarrassed, he plopped himself into the seat offered.

"What does my age matter?" Isbella spoke in hushed tones. She didn't exactly want to whisper, but she also didn't want any eavesdroppers either. "I have your money, just like we agreed. What's the big deal?"

"What's the big deal?! Listen here, girl, I'm already in trouble with the IRS about some . . . some misunderstandings."

A waft of pleasant cologne suddenly drifted toward Isabella. Was that Brad? Did he put that on just before he left his parent's basement?

Brad looked around, his eyes judging everyone. His voice got quieter. "I don't want to get caught dealing to minors."

Isabella's mouth hung open. Nothing was going to plan. And what was Brad talking about?! "I'm . . . I'm sorry. Are you Brad from Brad's Amazing Ender of the World Printing Service?" She blushed again.

"Yes! And here are the goods," Brad said, shoving the paper bag across the table. He immediately looked around again. "I mean, here's your 3D printout, just like you ordered."

Isbella wasn't sure if she wanted to look in the bag. It had dark grease spots on it and smelled like french fries. She began unrolling the top anyway. A bright yellow *M* logo revealed itself on the bag.

Isabella glanced around. She was going to pay close to two hundred dollars for something presented like this?!

Grace. *Grace!*

Isabella smiled at Brad.

Then she dared to look inside the bag.

27

CHAD FROZE.

The guard wasn't a typical museum guard. This was one of Ledger's mercs. A mercenary who sported a shiny bald head and wore a long, straight beard that hung down over his tactical vest. Cradled in his arms was an over/under shotgun. A Browning, by the look of it.

The light was still very dim, but Chad knew his rifles. He had used the Browning more times than he could count. At least, while playing *Rainbow Six*.

But by the way the guard strode casually through the gallery, he still hadn't seen Chad. It made sense. From where Chad was positioned, he was practically part of the exhibit.

Yet all of this caused a dilemma inside of Chad.

Because he still hadn't gotten his photo.

And he wanted it.

Badly.

All it would take was rotating his thumb. If he could just get it around to the front of his phone and—

Wait. Had Chad used the flash last time?

The guard approached. Was this guy ex-military? He looked it. But by the way he carried his shotgun high on his chest, the merc probably wasn't American-trained.

Weaving through the display, the guard aimlessly wandered closer and closer until—

He paused, taking a sudden interest in a rather frightening display of ancient Japanese masks. Faces of red devils with pronounced frowns. As he gazed at the display, the guard's back slowly rotated toward Chad.

This was Chad's chance!

Chad flipped on his phone, immediately tapping on the camera app.

And for a moment, Chad's face became bathed in light, illuminated by the screen! He immediately yanked the phone down, hiding it behind the suit of armor.

Chad smashed buttons. He frantically swiped down, and then up again, trying to find the brightness level adjustment.

Whoever made this confounded operating system clearly didn't know good design if it bit them in the rear! Who would bury that setting?! Clearly, they had no idea how phones were used in the real world!

The guard suddenly turned back around.

Fortunately, Chad's phone dimmed . . . and then shut off.

A new thought came flooding into Chad's mind.

What were the chances that maybe the guard would take the photo for him?

No. You can't ask the guard.

Yes, he might get a better photo. But no, Chad should definitely NOT ask. Especially when he was someplace he shouldn't be. Yes, of course Chad knew that. But he just had to run the idea up the mental flagpole to see if anyone saluted.

A new idea!

One Chad simply couldn't decide if it was good or bad.

And he didn't have the time to debate it. Because in ten feet, the guard would be on him!

Eight feet.

Six feet.

So, why not? Chad's curiosity said it was a good idea. And that seemed like a good argument.

Maybe if Chad couldn't get a photo of himself—

He'd get a photo of the guard!

As fast as lightning, Chad's camera was up and pointed.

CLICK!

The camera flash exploded with light!

The guard stumbled backward, covering his eyes. Blinded.

Chad took that moment to do the best and wisest thing he could possibly think of doing in a dangerous situation.

No, not run. Chad tugged on the handle of a samurai sword.

SCHWING!

And since the hilt felt *so* good in his hands, he couldn't resist adding to it. Chad yanked a samurai helmet off a nearby table.

The guard blinked repeatedly. He lifted his shotgun, hiding behind it. The tip of the rifle wandering aimlessly.

Chad leaned in a bit.

Somewhere Chad felt like he had dreamt of this moment.

For most of his life.

Or at least for the last ten seconds.

"Join me, and together we can rule the galaxy as father and son!"

KR-BLAMM! BLAMM!

The gunfire went wide, missing Chad completely. The steel shot slammed into a nearby display. Bamboo and leather armor splintered, erupting into the air.

"It is useless to resist!"

The guard pumped his rifle.

BLAMM, BLAMM!

The shots decimated a display of ceremonial cleansing bowls. A spray of glass and porcelain showered them both.

"Yes, your thoughts betray you," Chad coughed. He probably couldn't keep up the lowered voice for much longer.

That, and the guard blinked less. His face looked intense. His eyes were dark and focused. Had his vision returned?

Hmm . . .

Maybe this was a good time to run.

28

ANIKA SLIPPED BEHIND AN unmanned forklift. Robin had stayed back, crouching in the shadows.

If there was a person to go sneaking, it was probably her. Anika had taken several years of ballet and gymnastics. Mostly, she remembered sore feet and aching muscles. But the classes weren't a complete waste. They did give Anika a sense of her body and its movement that the others didn't have.

Anika wove on light feet past a stack of museum benches.

She was curious. All she wanted was a quick peek inside the crates.

She continued to work her way toward the end of the line of crates yet to be loaded. A few at the very back still sat open. Maybe if she got a look in one of them, things would make more sense.

A worker approached, carrying a large frame wrapped in canvas.

Anika clung to her little patch of darkness, waiting. Timing it. As the worker passed, Anika rotated around an empty pedestal, careful to stay hidden.

SQUEAK, SQUEAK.

In the distance, another worker drew near, pushing a large cart that had one bad wheel.

In order to get a closer look at the crates, Anika needed to cross the walkway. How could she do this? If she went too early, the cart pusher might see Anika. If she waited too long, the frame carrier might return.

Not yet.

Not yet.

NOW.

Anika stepped forward just as another worker appeared. This worker busied themselves with what was on their clipboard.

ABORT! Anika spun around and ducked back into her hiding spot.

Had they seen her? Did she even dare poke her head out to look?

Instead, Anika listened. The worker's footsteps continued on pace. No one stopped. No one moved into a run. That was good news, wasn't it?

Was there ever going to be a break in the steady stream of museum employees?

Or was there another way?

Anika looked up.

It wasn't pretty, but it might work. There had to be thirty feet of industrial shelving above her. It extended up past where the lights cast their illumination.

Could she cross over at the top of the shelves?

She would have to jump across the aisle. How wide was that exactly?

It was too hard to tell from where Anika was. She would have to get closer. But it didn't look that far.

Anika *really* wanted that closer look.

She slipped back toward the outer walls. She would climb the shelving as far away from the workers as possible. That way, if she made any sounds, she had the best chances of being undetected.

Anika looked at her hands. She wished she had gymnastic chalk, but she'd have to make do. Anika jumped up and caught the lip of the shelf above her. She did a pull-up, swinging one leg up, and then finished hoisting herself into place.

The shelf was packed with boxes, all neatly labeled. Anika used the sturdiest-looking one to help climb up to the next level of shelving.

Making progress wasn't that challenging. It sort of reminded Anika of the playgrounds her parents took her to when she was younger. Granted, this playground didn't have any wood chips below. It only had concrete to catch her if she fell.

Like a nimble cat burglar, Anika made her way to the top.

The dust lay thick here atop the boxes. Anika covered her mouth and nose. She couldn't afford to cough. Or worse, sneeze!

Bathed in darkness, Anika inched her way around the last few boxes. She stood at the edge, looking down at the aisle. It was good she had climbed up to the very top. Because now there were more workers. All of them moving busily down below.

Anika looked across the aisle to the shelves on the other side.

They looked just as stable as the ones she had climbed, didn't they?

Only, now that she stood at the gap, they looked *much* further away.

Had it been an optical illusion from down below? There was no way she could jump this . . . could she? But what other options did she have?

Anika backed up. She quietly rearranged some boxes as she went, clearing them from her way.

Anika would need as long and as clear a running area as she could get.

But was this long enough?

Don't overthink it, she told herself. This was like standing on the high dive. If you didn't simply jump, you never would.

Anika lowered herself into a sprinter's stance.

And ran!

29

Isabella gasped.

The 3D-printed diamond was stunning!

Did it even sparkle inside the bag? Maybe Isabella had misjudged Brad. This diamond looked just like the photos Robin had sent her. The beauty wasn't because of her modeling skills. Brad was an artist!

Isabella reached in and pulled the replica out of the bag.

The edges of the print caught the light from above her. The jewel almost looked like it had come alive. Self-illuminated! When—

Brad's hand rudely shoved the diamond back into the bag. "What are you doing?!" he hissed. "*Don't* pull it out!"

"What? Why?" Isabella coughed.

And then Brad did something even more shocking. He grabbed the McDonald's bag, yanking it right out of her hand. "I'm sorry. This isn't going to work."

Brad thrust his seat back, causing it to grate on the floor. He got up and started to leave.

"No, wait. I'm sorry," Isabella said, trying to use a soothing voice. "I honestly don't know what came over me. I don't know what I was thinking. Please. Please sit back down."

Brad frowned. But he also didn't move any closer toward the door.

"I have the money," Isabella whispered.

Brad frowned even more, anxiously looking around.

Maybe she shouldn't have spoken about the money. Or maybe that was what was keeping Brad from leaving. How was Isabella supposed to know?!

But at last, Brad slouched back into his seat again.

Isabella pulled out a stack of cash from her pocket. She was about to hand it over when—

"Under the table," Brad said through clenched teeth. "Thank you very much."

Isabella felt confused. Was she doing something illegal? She slipped the money under the table.

"Can I ask you a question, Brad?" she asked as he quietly thumbed through the bills. Her question must have interrupted him, because he grimaced and started over with counting.

"Am I missing something here? Why are we doing this transaction so secretively?" Isabella whispered. "Are we breaking some law that I don't know about?"

Brad glanced up. He looked like he was about to explain something to a kindergartener. "Um, hello? How do I know what you're going to do with that *hamburger*?" At the last word, Brad nodded to the bag that now sat awkwardly between them. "You're a minor, so that means *I'm* the one who's going to go to jail when *you* do something stupid with it. What happens if you try to swallow it, huh? What if you choke on it and die, huh?! What then?"

Isabella blinked a few times.

"Brad, give me a little grace, will you? What if I promise I'm not going to swallow it?" Isabella held up two fingers. "Scout's honor."

"Oh, really? Then what *are* you going to do with it? And don't you dare lie to me! I want the truth."

Isabella hesitated, scratching her one leg with the other. She should never have left the trailer. This was definitely NOT worth it.

She could tell Brad a lie. Just a little one. It wouldn't count. Not really.

Instead, Isabella leaned forward and stared Brad straight in the eyes.

"Brad, my friends and I work for the FBI. And right now, as we speak, we're breaking into the Museum of Arts and Culture next door with plans to swap your little *hamburger* for a real *Big Mac.*"

Brad didn't react.

Was he still processing all of that information? What was he thinking?!

Brad leaned back in his chair. Somehow, he looked relieved.

"Okay," he said, nodding. "I'm alright with that. Just promise me you won't light it on fire or stick it up your nose."

Now it was Isabella's turn to stay cool and collected.

"Brad . . . I give you my word."

30

CHAD RAN!

He sidestepped the samurai sandal display just as it burst apart.

BLAMM!

Shards of glass and ancient culture littered the area.

The warm glow of an exit light shone ahead. Chad changed direction, sprinting for it.

He could hear the guard behind him pumping another cartridge into the chamber. Chad dropped to the ground, sliding under a display. Destruction followed.

BLAMM! BLAMM!

Chad jumped back to his feet. Using a zigzag pattern, he vaulted a glass case just as it dissolved underneath him from a shotgun blast. He wasn't going to make it to the exit in time. It was simply too far!

KR-CLICK!

Chad heard the new sound behind him. One he knew all too well.

The guard was out of ammo. That was the sound of a Browning over/under looking for the next cartridge that wasn't there.

Chad stopped on a dime.

He calmly turned around. Sure enough, the mercenary scrambled, yanking more shotgun shells out of his belt.

Chad didn't rush things. If real life was anything like *Rainbow Six* on the PS2, Chad had plenty of time. He began walking back toward the guard.

Chad's calm and deliberate approach only made the guard fumble more. One shell and then another slipped out of his hands. Right now, he only had about a 30 percent chance of getting one into the shotgun. The others bounced on the floor.

Chad glanced to his side. He reached out and randomly grabbed something. It was a tiny statue of a horse mid-gallop. It felt heavy. Solid lead.

Time slowed.

And just as the tip of the shotgun rose again—

A wide grin growing across the guard's face—

Chad lofted the hefty statue skyward. It arced up toward the ceiling.

Chad didn't slow his approach. Instead he squinted, spying the confusion on the guard's face. How many times had Chad used this tactic on the playground? By now, it was a classic. Toss a lunchbox or a school book while approaching the bully. It worked every time! Well, *nearly* every time. Forcing the other to decide between fight or flight. Between high and low. Between this and that.

Sure enough, the merc froze. Caught in the decision.

The merc took a step back.

Or he tried, except he stepped on one of his own shotgun shells. His foot slipped.

KR-BLAMM!

The shot went wide. Ceiling plaster rained down in chunks.

THWACK!

It was a fraction of a second between fates for the guard. It was either his head connecting with the hardwood flooring or the all-too-solid lead horse that got him. Either way, the guard slumped into unconsciousness.

Time resumed.

Chad dusted off his hands. He looked around. He had work to do and now he was behind schedule. If Robin or Anika knew anything about what had just happened, Chad would have probably gotten a lecture. He didn't need one. He knew what he had to do now—pick up the pace. Move double-time. After all, Sneaky, Inc. was on an important mission.

Only there was *one* more important thing Chad had to attend to first.

Chad climbed back onto the chair behind the suit of samurai armor and held out his phone.

CLICK!

31

ANIKA FELT HER BODY become weightless!

She had leaped between the shelves. With the ceiling lights below her, it was a challenge to see her target. Did she have enough speed?

Anika stretched her legs out forward. Reaching.

YES!

Both of her feet connected with the shelving. She had done it! A jump longer than she thought she could make. And a solid landing!

Only her forward momentum carried her too far. She tried to stop her body with her hands. Instead, she collided with a pile of museum boxes. The uppermost box wobbled, teetering on the edge.

Anika thrust out both of her hands to catch it—

Too late!

No, this couldn't be happening! Not to her. She watched as the box somersaulted.

On its descent, it clipped the edge of one shelf—

BANG!

Which sent the box spinning into a neighboring shelf.

BANG, CLANG, BONK!

Ugh, ouch, rats! Did it really have to hit everything on its way down? Apparently, yes.

SMASSHHH!

Upon hitting the floor, the box split open. Its fragile contents splayed across the floor.

At least three workers immediately spun. All work at loading the crates stopped. Flashlights flicked on. Attention was first given to the contents spilled over the floor. But quickly enough, the workers rotated their beams upward.

By then, Anika wasn't there.

She knew a little bit about human nature. First, you look at what made the noise, and then you turn your attention to where it came from. And what caused it.

Anika had already removed herself from view. She was three shelves away by now. The jump between neighboring shelves was close. Easy compared to the leap across the aisle. With the help of gravity, Anika silently dropped from one shelf to the next.

She alighted on the ground in a crouch. Now was her chance. With the guards distracted, she could get a view inside the crates. The ones that lay before her still had not been sealed.

Anika couldn't take long digging through them. Instead, she pulled out her phone. With one eye on the workers, Anika took a series of photos without aiming, merely holding the phone over the crates.

She got shots inside of at least three crates and didn't want to risk more. Looking both ways, Anika ducked across the aisle and slipped back into the shadows.

Anika couldn't help herself. She chose a path close to a few of the workers who were still examining the fallen box. She faintly heard them say something about a squirrel that must have somehow gotten inside.

Anika continued on, smirking.

Sure enough, Robin was still where she had left him, huddling in a small nook between storage boxes.

"You certainly made enough noise," Robin whispered.

Was he offering his lop-sided smile when he said that? It was too dark to tell. Anika hunkered down beside him. She selected all of her new photos and air-dropped them to Robin's phone.

They both flipped through the images.

Artwork filled the crates. Paintings, statues, mosaics, all sorts. Why was Ledger moving all this artwork?

Anika picked one painting at random. With a Google image match, she quickly found the artist's name. Then, doing another search, she looked to see if the artwork was going out on loan for an exhibit at any other museums soon.

It wasn't.

"If you owned a museum," Anika whispered, "why would you want to move so much of the art? All on the same day?"

Dimly lit by his phone, Robin tilted his head. "And why would you do it at night, especially during a busy gala with so many important guests?"

"I don't know." Anika shook her head as their eyes connected. "I just looked up traffic camera feeds in the area. These trucks have been coming and going for the past few days."

"Ledger's up to something."

Anika's brow lowered. She knew Robin, and she knew what he would say next.

"And we have to find out what it is."

32

BACK INSIDE THE TRAILER, Isabella clipped the McDonald's bag to the bottom of a drone.

BZZZZRRR!

Its tiny propellers jumped to life, and the drone slowly lifted from her hand. It drifted up and out through the ceiling hatch.

Isabella had preprogrammed the drone. Like an Amazon delivery drone, it would follow the boys' route like a GPS signal, through the rooftop ventilation shaft and into the building. It would even prompt her for remote assistance if it ran into any problems.

Isabella flopped back down into her seat.

DING. A text from Robin. He wanted to see the guest list—those invited to the gala by this mysterious Mr. Smith.

Isabella began to type on her keyboard, but then hesitated.

That voice—the one she had heard over the walkie-talkie that day behind the grocery store—she knew it from somewhere. It had been scratchy and hard to hear. But she just couldn't get it out of her head. Was it a teacher from her old school? Maybe a guidance counselor?

It didn't matter. Not really. Isabella's fingers began typing again. She enjoyed the challenge of hacking into a new component of the museum's computer system. It was a chess match with their security team. Every time they locked the system down harder and tighter, Isabella only found another way in.

She did a few searches through the code. Surely they would keep digital records of those who were invited.

With a little digging, Isabella found something. Yes, this was it!

She scrolled through it. Names, names, and more names. She didn't recognize any of them.

Command + A: Isabella selected all the names. Command + C, and then Command + V: She copied and pasted them into her own spreadsheet. She would write a small script. Something to help her dig up information off the web about each name. Places like LinkedIn and Facebook would be a good start. Maybe if she had time, she might even run them through IRS.gov and take a peek under the hood.

Isabella didn't know a Mr. Smith, did she? Maybe that was the librarian back in her old town. But he didn't sound like that . . . did he?

A new thought suddenly flashed into her mind. An ugly thought.

Hold on. Robin wouldn't have lied to her . . . would he?!

Robin examined the museum map on his phone. He overlaid the first floor map onto an architectural drawing of the basement. He had found the old blueprints buried on the city bureau's website while Anika was busy climbing. The image was low resolution, but it was good enough for Robin to get the general sense of where they were.

"I want to see something," Robin whispered. "Just ahead. It's a mistake on the map or—" Robin didn't finish his thought. It had to be an error. Or else, something completely unusual.

Robin and Anika made their way well past all the workers and shelves.

This section of the basement sat mostly empty. Empty and dark.

Was it an older part of the building?

Sure, there was the odd piece or two of museum furniture. They sat like abandoned monuments in an otherwise vast and empty space.

Robin wanted to turn on his phone light. But there really was little need. From what dim light there was, he could see that there was nothing to trip over. His footsteps, as quiet as they were, echoed. It sounded eerie enough that it caused Robin to breathe more shallowly.

There was nothing else except for something fifty yards ahead. A giant igloo? That was the best Robin could describe it. A concrete-looking dome sat in the middle of the open stretch of nothing. A small pinpoint light from one side of it offered the only illumination.

According to the map, the igloo sat exactly beneath the Star of Flame Diamond. But the concrete dome wasn't on the original blueprints.

Exchanging glances, Robin and Anika both held back.

Should they approach the dome?

What was it? After looking around, Robin flicked on his phone light. He shielded it with one hand, directing the beam.

The dome must have been about fifteen feet high. The walls were gently sloped—enough that climbing up them would likely be tricky, but not impossible.

Anika reached out and touched it.

Robin followed her lead. It *felt* like concrete, smooth and cold. The structure was likely poured in place, since Robin couldn't find any seams.

How wide was this thing? It was hard to tell, but Robin guessed it might be thirty feet.

Robin gestured to Anika. The two of them split up, each slowly pacing around opposite sides of the structure.

Alone, Robin lifted his light upward. The ceiling was too high to see. But a slight reflection revealed a set of several thick pipes connecting the dome to the roof above. Were those wide enough for a human to fit through?

Robin approached the light mounted on the side of the dome. He inched forward.

A security keypad.

Was this the entrance to the igloo structure? Sure enough, on the other side of the keypad, a steel door presented itself. It looked thick and offered no windows.

Anika approached from the opposite side.

"Reach out to Izzy," Robin whispered. His voice sounded hollow in such a large chamber. "Let's see if we can get this thing open."

33

ANIKA WHISPERED TO ISABELLA, "How's it going out there?"

"Not bad. I got to meet Brad from Brad's Amazing Ender of the World Printing Service." Isabella laughed. "So that made things interesting."

"Brad's Amazing what?"

"Don't ask." Anika could hear Isabella's keyboard clicking. "Okay, I've got you the number. Type this in: 55-73-23-23."

Anika typed in each set of numbers. As soon as the last number cleared, a green light blinked on.

Anika stood back as the steel door began to move. That's when she noticed the groves and gears built into the floor. The door ground open, slow and steady, like a bulldozer. Placing a hand on it, Anika felt the power in the mechanism. Someone had engineered the door to open no matter what, clearing aside anything that might be in its way.

"That work?" Isabella asked.

"Uh-huh. Nice work."

"Thanks. Oh, and you and Robin should get a little takeout any moment."

"Wait, you got us food?"

"Not exactly. Oh, and you *have* to promise me you won't try to eat it or shove it up your nose, alright?"

"Um, okay. I'm not sure we're in the habit of doing that with things, but whatever."

The gentle whine of Isabella's drone suddenly became louder. Robin shined his light up, catching sight of it. As it descended, Robin unclipped the McDonald's bag from underneath it.

So, Isabella hadn't been joking? She actually had bought food from—

Robin pulled out the printed diamond. His phone light caused it to sparkle.

"Wow," Anika said, reaching out as Robin handed her the diamond. As he folded up the drone, Anika fingered the replica. She turned it over and over. It was stunning. "Nice work again, Izzy."

"Thank you. I'll pass on your appreciation to Brad—you know, if we ever meet again. Which I sincerely hope we *never* do."

The girls laughed as Anika bagged the diamond.

She turned her attention back to the dome. Anika ducked and followed Robin inside.

Unbelievable! Anika was not expecting what she saw. Inside was a furnished apartment of sorts. It was snug, but very liveable and classy. It had a version of all the amenities you would want to live comfortably. A small kitchenette, including a sink and a microwave. A lovely couch and working LED lamps on both sides. On the other side of the room sat several bookshelves and a single bed, neatly made.

Anika shared a look of surprise with Robin.

She approached an open door and glanced inside. Within was a bathroom, including a toilet and a little shower. It was no bigger than what an RV would be outfitted with.

Everything was there to make a complete set of living quarters.

But why? Who would ever want to live here? In an apartment buried in the dark and creepy part of a museum basement?

Anika opened the mini-fridge. Someone had packed it with food. Premade meals, all neatly organized and sorted. Untouched.

"Have you ever seen anything like this?" Anika asked.

Robin didn't answer. He only shook his head in disbelief as he examined a bookshelf.

Anika approached the front door again. What a creation! The door had to be close to six inches thick, made of reinforced steel. And the igloo walls were close to a foot and a half deep themselves. The place looked like a bunker for the end of the world.

But why? It didn't make sense. None of it did. The fridge was only stocked with a week's worth of food. Maybe two weeks, if you rationed it. How could that feed anyone for long enough to survive a world-ending disaster?

Or maybe it didn't need to.

34

CHAD USED THE FIND My app to track Robin and Anika.

It was seriously creepy down in the basement. Especially in this section. Why was it so empty? Someone needed to pay the electric bill, apparently. It was dark as sin down here.

Anika's long duffel bag was getting heavy. Chad slung it over his other shoulder.

He looked at his phone again. Either Chad was seriously lost, or the other two were inside the giant doghouse up ahead.

It wasn't a doghouse, right? Nobody made doghouses that big. Well, Chad had a neighbor once whose doghouse sorta looked like that: like a plastic bubble sinking into the ground. Only, the neighbors kept a nasty, snarling Doberman chained up to theirs. The dog had ended up dragging the doghouse behind him all across his yard. He needed one like this. Gigantic!

Chad approached the open door, ducking inside.

"Surprise!" he yelled for effect.

By the look on Robin's face and the fact that Anika was now clutching her heart, maybe he had startled them.

"Why do you have to *do* that?!" Anika growled, trying to catch her breath.

"Seriously," Robin hissed. "You do know you have an earpiece, right? You are allowed to use it to tell us that you're close."

"Right. I forgot about that," Chad said, throwing himself down on the bed.

It wasn't until his head hit the super-fluffy pillow that he even started to wonder why there was a bed inside the giant doghouse.

"Don't sit on that!" Anika yelled. "We haven't checked for traps!"

"Fine!" Chad complained, slowly getting up. "I know when I'm not appreciated." Chad started opening one cabinet after another. "Is there any food in here? 'Cause I didn't get a chance to snag anything back with the caterer, if you can believe that. They had all this wonderful food, and I didn't take any of it. I didn't get distracted. Are you proud of me? I went straight to Anika's bag hidden under crates of onions—nice hiding spot, by the way—and I came right here. No stops. No dillydallying."

Chad paused, waiting for praise.

Only it never came.

Oh, what was this? He opened the mini-fridge. Chad pulled out a plastic container of food and began microwaving it.

"WHAT ARE YOU DOING?!" Robin yelled. "This isn't your personal cafeteria, Chad. You can't just go eating everything in front of you. You know that?! Actually, Chad, why don't you make yourself useful? Go and stand by that wall." Robin pointed.

"Can I at least take this with me? I think it's spaghetti."

Chad didn't get an answer. And by the matching looks on their faces, he could assume that meant no.

Chad slunk over to an empty wall. Honestly, he felt like kicking something. He was in time-out and he knew it!

Why wasn't he appreciated?! He did as much work as the others. Yes, he did! So then why was he being treated like a child?!

Chad tugged on one ear, bending it down further than it already was.

That's when he saw it.

A bright red button.

It sat mounted on the wall. Not far away.

It looked shiny and pleasantly round.

No. Chad turned away. He knew he shouldn't touch it. He knew what trouble it would likely cause. Besides, Chad was tired of getting yelled at.

Chad turned back around.

Why did that button look so doggone pushable?

Like it actually *wanted* to be pressed!

Thankfully, Chad had the necessary willpower *not* to press the button.

But apparently his finger didn't.

It pressed the button!

35

ALARMS BLARED!

Robin clamped both hands over his ears. He spun around, trying to figure out what had gone wrong. What mistake the team had made. His first thought was to accuse Chad of something. Anything!

Chad shrugged. "I didn't do it," he said, innocently enough.

Then why was Chad hiding his hands behind his back? Robin's brow lowered. Somehow, Chad didn't look innocent. All Robin knew was that Chad had better *not* be lying. Not to him!

"We gotta get out of here!" Anika yelled over the alarm.

But then everyone stopped.

A small hatch in the ceiling hinged open. A clear plexiglass tube extended downward. It wasn't very large, maybe ten inches wide, and it continued lowering until it was only a few feet off the ground.

What was this?

A small trapdoor in the side of the plexiglass tube presented itself.

Should Robin open it? Would it shut off the alarm? What if there was a poisonous gas inside? No, that didn't make any sense.

And suddenly a package slid down the tube. Was this vacuum-controlled? Like the deposit tubes at a bank drive-through?

Yet this package was nothing as crude as a twist-lid container with deposit slips and a lollipop. A deep blue satin pillow, trimmed in gold, had lowered into place beside the trapdoor. And nestled neatly in its center sat something that looked like . . . like . . .

The Star of Flame Diamond!

Robin blinked.

How could this possibly be real?

Nobody moved. Robin snapped open the trapdoor. Reaching inside, he pulled out the diamond. Robin held it like it was a live grenade. He looked up at the others, as stunned as if he had just been visited by an angel.

Anika scrambled for the McDonald's bag, swiping it off the dining room table. She pulled out the 3D-printed copy and paced closer to Robin.

The two diamonds came together. One very real, and the other very fake.

Sitting side by side, Isabella's 3D print no longer looked that amazing. If anything, it looked like the cheap imposter that it was.

Holding the priceless diamond in his hands had somehow mesmerized Robin. Somewhere he had lost focus on the alarms, even though they were still ringing. Anika touched him on the arm and Robin looked up and away, snapping out of it.

"This must be the safety vault for the diamond," Robin yelled. "When something triggers the alarms, the system automatically sends it down here for protection. Into this vault or this . . ." Robin glanced around at the apartment. "This bunker of sorts."

Anika looked up. "But how did it get sent down here? What triggered it?"

"Um," Chad said, scratching himself randomly. "I might know something about that."

Eyes bored holes into Chad when he sheepishly pointed to a button on the wall.

"Wait. You actually pressed it?!"

"Is that a technical question or just a hypothetical—"

"Unbelievable!" Robin yelled, shaking his head. "And for once, it might have actually worked out okay."

"Really? You think so?" Chad asked, rubbing his hands together. "Do I get a reward or something?"

Robin swapped the diamonds. He paused just long enough to answer: "No!" Robin dropped the genuine diamond into the McDonald's bag while he slipped the fake onto the blue satin bed.

Without hesitation, Robin shut the trapdoor and reached over to whack the red button again.

Sure enough, the alarms stopped. The pillow and the fake diamond quivered, then rose up, getting sucked back into the ceiling. Stepping back, Robin watched the plexiglass tube retract.

"Amazing."

The ceiling hatch hinged closed, becoming nearly invisible again.

The silence felt significant, especially in contrast to all the noise only moments ago.

Chad cleared his throat. "Is this a bad time to mention that I've made other oopsies before that have actually ended up helping the group? I just wanted to make that clear for the record, you know? You made it sound like this was the first time."

36

"ROBIN, WE GOTTA GO!" Anika said before darting back outside the bunker.

Robin smoothed out the bedcovers. He wanted everything to look like it used to. Like they had never been there.

Robin stood back, taking in the entire apartment. He knew they had little time. Someone would have to research what tripped the alarm. There was every reason to assume a wave of security was already on its way.

But Robin couldn't help grinning to himself. He felt pleased. They had done it! Again.

And it hadn't even been that much of a challenge!

Sneaky, Inc. had gone above and beyond. His FBI handlers would have to be pleased now, wouldn't they? When push came to shove, Robin and his team had not only gotten the photos, but the diamond itself. And that had to say something about their skills, didn't it?

Robin hunched over and ducked out through the steel doorway. He pressed a few buttons on the security keypad. Out of the corner of his eye, he watched as the door ground closed.

With this mission practically finished, Sneaky, Inc. was ready for primetime. For bigger missions and bigger rewards! Sure, the team still had a few minor issues to iron out. Like Chad lying to the group. If they were going to work as a team, Robin would have to dole out some discipline for that. Make Chad an example to the others. But that could come later. After they had a chance to enjoy their success.

Smiling, Robin slipped on his backpack. Anika and Chad were a good distance ahead. Robin didn't mind. What at first had felt like an eerie part of the museum basement now felt known. It felt like something he had conquered. Like the mighty warriors of old, Robin had once again vanquished the mighty monster. Ledger the Terrible!

I want you to tell her the truth.

Seriously? Why would the whisper come at a time like this? That voice in his head couldn't really be the Holy Spirit, could it? The team had just won—another victory! Telling Isabella now would only sabotage the celebration, wouldn't it? Robin could always wait for a better time. Maybe back at their headquarters in the old grocery store. If they were all hyped from celebrating, she wouldn't think it was a big deal then. Especially if *he* didn't make it a big deal.

Robin pressed his earpiece. "Isabella, get ready for extraction."

"Really? You got it? You swapped out the real diamond?"

"Yup. Oh, and I think you have a few bugs in your alarm program. I thought you said it was working, but clearly we found the exception."

"I'm sorry. Yeah, I should have said that it was *nearly* working. Sorry about that."

Robin shook his head.

She had lied to him too, short and simple.

Better not to make too much of it here and now, or he would have to bring up the incident with Chad as well.

"No worries. We'll talk about it later. Over and out."

A new set of thoughts came over him. If Isabella lied about her software, what else was she lying about? What about the others? Was Anika telling him the truth about everything? What about Chad? Well, Chad was a permanent question mark. With Chad, you simply had to learn how to work with what you had.

But the questions continued nagging Robin. He really didn't need this now. He'd address the group's rather blatant honesty issues in a meeting some other time.

Robin pushed away the thoughts as he broke into a jog—

Trying to catch up with the others.

37

SITTING AT THE MOBILE command desk, Isabella tapped a pencil.

She didn't really have anything else to do. Her new program collecting data on the evening's guests was running in the background. And there really wasn't much need to fix Project Alarm Mute now that the mission was done. Isabella could always figure out that glitch after school sometime, when she was bored.

TAP, TAP, TAP.

Isabella's pencil stopped. She pulled up a browser window.

No better time to shop!

She flipped through formal gown options. They were all from the local shops in town. Getting a glance at what the gala attendees wore that evening had piqued her interest. You know, just a little.

That and the idea of actually attending that evening's gala. Even though it seemed like a dream.

Of course, Isabella would never actually do it. She wasn't stupid. And she knew the risks involved. But . . . it wouldn't be hard to add a fake name to the digital registry. And she could always Photoshop an invitation if she really needed one.

She was only missing the dress.

It would have to be a stunning gown, because even if she slipped inside just for a peek—which she would never do!—she'd have to look gorgeous.

Just like the dress in front of her. Wow! It was simply stunning. A long crimson gown with a small splash of sequins—it would look amazing with her long dark hair. It was pricey, but Isabella had the money in her account. And she could always return the dress the next day. Or was that cheating?

No, all of this was foolish.

Isabella minimized the browser and stood up.

What she really needed was to stretch her legs—to think about something else.

Although . . .

Isabella leaned over and flipped the browser back open.

She couldn't leave the trailer during a mission. Not for a dress! Maybe for a 3D-printed diamond, but not a ballgown. That would be practically treasonous. She would have to face the firing squad if she did that.

But if she had a minute or two inside the gala, she might also catch a glimpse of this elusive Mr. Smith. Once and for all, she could put her questions about recognizing his voice to rest.

"Hmm," Isabella said aloud. She went back to tapping her pencil. "I wonder if Uber could actually deliver a gown to a parked trailer?"

38

WHAT WAS THEIR PLAN now? Robin brainstormed how to exfil the team safely. Leaving through the basement garage wasn't a great option—too many guards and workers. Maybe if they had a distraction, they could get out through there. It certainly was the closest exit. Otherwise, they were going to have to sneak past all the crates again and hope that they—

Robin heard the engines roar before he could see them. His fears had come true.

Four black SUVs careened down the basement ramp. Screeching to a stop, the vehicles entirely blocked the exit.

Ledger's elite team of mercenaries poured out of the vehicles. Dressed entirely in dark colors, the mercs were battle-ready. They wore advanced kevlar helmets and vests and tight-fitting combat boots. Their weapons looked illegal and likely supplied off the black market.

Hunched over, their rifle tips hunting side to side, the kill squad advanced. "Get down! GET DOWN!" several mercenaries shouted.

The invading army of at least twenty mercs took the workers by surprise. Screams and cries echoed off the walls. The mercs shoved the workers to the ground, disregarding any valuable artwork in the process.

Some mercs were zip-tying the workers' hands behind their backs. They weren't taking any chances. Weaving through the bodies that now littered the floor, the rest of the kill squad fanned out.

So much for sneaking through.

Hiding behind some crates, Robin scanned the cavernous darkness behind him. There was no way out that direction. Only the bunker. Could the team go back and lock themselves in? The igloo certainly could withstand any firepower the merc threw at it. But then again, the mercs would have Robin's team trapped!

No, there had to be another way.

That's when Robin saw a narrow hallway. It led away from the basement garage doors. To an office area, maybe? Possibly the workrooms for the archival staff who maintained the artwork in storage. And with any luck, there might be a back exit.

Robin tapped Anika and Chad on the shoulders. Using hand signals, he gestured to their new destination.

Slipping forward, the three teammates used the cover from the crates and shelving. Clinging to the shadows, they approached the entrance to the hallway.

Only, a handful of mercs were also approaching this area of the basement. Their rifles scanned back and forth continuously for any movement.

Robin paused. Ahead, there was no more cover for getting into the hallway. The last ten yards were completely out in the open. They would have to make a run for it. But this was too much space to cross unnoticed. It wouldn't work. Not with the mercs' fingers already on the triggers.

Robin glanced beside him, inside an open half-sized crate.

The label on the lid read: MING DYNASTY VASE. TAKE EX-TREME CARE!

Sure enough, a long white vase lay inside, decorated with fine blue flowers interwoven with a Chinese dragon. Robin plucked the artifact out of its straw bedding.

Robin held up three fingers.

Two fingers.

One.

Cringing just a little, Robin threw the vase. Up and over his head, the precious ceramic flew in a high arc.

The group ran!

SMASHHH!

Nothing short of twenty rifles suddenly swiveled. All of them now pointed toward the sound.

But one merc must have gotten wise. He pivoted.

Bringing up the rear, Robin nearly made it into the hallway when—

BRAPP! BRAPP!

Chunks of concrete and rubble clobbered Robin as he spun around the corner. He continued to sprint past Anika and Chad. Both of the others had paused at the entry, waiting. And just as

Robin sped past, they pushed. Several tall shelves teetered and toppled over. A clatter of books, paperwork, and shelving now barred the way.

It wasn't much of a deterrent. The mercs would be over it in seconds. But Robin and his team could use *every* second they could get.

The team raced down the hallway. Triggered by motion sensors, office lights began blinking on. But the lights were taking forever to brighten! Cleary a much older technology.

The team rounded the first corner.

Robin tried the first door. Locked. He rammed his face against the office windows. He couldn't see much through the dim haze. Was there a way out inside?

Nothing.

Robin tried the next office. Painting restoration. No exits.

"Come on, let's get deeper in!" he yelled to the others, glancing over his shoulder.

Surely they had to have a back staircase. Didn't basic fire safety require that?!

But if there was an emergency exit, Robin and his team couldn't find it.

Robin did a double-take as he passed a small staff break room. Were those donuts on the table? Robin shot a quick look back at Anika. "Don't let Chad in there."

Frustrated, Robin pressed on.

The place was an absolute maze. And claustrophobic too! Hallways led in every direction. Little offices littered the area, each one focusing on different services. Here was a room dedicated to four-teenth-century history books. Another one for X-raying paintings for any hidden work lying beneath the surface.

But no staircase!

"Here. Over here!" Chad yelled.

Where was his voice coming from?

Robin turned yet another corner and spied Chad waving his arms frantically.

"It's an elevator, I think."

Anika and Robin raced over to find Chad standing before an ancient freight elevator.

"Do you think I should press this button?"

Robin had to bite his tongue. He had to do something to prevent the absolutely terrible sarcastic words that came to mind. Instead, Robin calmly replied, "Yes, that would be helpful. Thank you." Although Robin didn't wait for Chad before he jabbed at the elevator button himself.

The group all stared at the doors, which did nothing.

Robin pressed the button again. And then about fifty more times.

They just had to wait.

But Robin could hear the mercs' footsteps approaching.

39

Robin glanced at his watch. He wiped his forehead with a sleeve. Spinning toward his friend, Robin forced a smile. "Can I ask you a question, Chad? Why is it you don't have any problems hitting a mystery button that you found on a bunker wall, but when it comes to something useful—like, I don't know, calling the elevator to save us from a bunch of guys who want to kill us!—you have to wait and ask permission?"

Robin jabbed the button again repeatedly.

"You know, that's a good question. If I write that series of business books, maybe I'll get into that."

"What? What does pressing buttons have to do with business?!" Robin growled, looking around him. Something had to be done. Any second, the mercs would turn the corner and they would be sitting ducks.

Robin spied a statue nearby. Lifesize, it sat on a rolling cart. The statue was pure white marble, fashioned in the shape of a lady holding shafts of wheat. But it was her clothing that was most remarkable. She wore a long, flowing gown that looked nearly real, frozen in time.

Jabbing the elevator button again, Robin could *finally* hear the squeaking and groaning of the gears inside. At least it was working. But would it ever actually arrive?!

At the end of the long hallway, the lights suddenly began flickering on again. It was an eerie sight, as if a ghost was triggering them. The mercs were just around the corner!

Robin grabbed the statue cart. With all his might, he dragged it in front of them. It wouldn't have been so difficult except for one wheel that wanted to go in a different direction!

Finally, he had it positioned in front of the elevator, and the three of them immediately jumped behind the statue—all lining up in a row. Just as Robin caught a glimpse of a rifle pointing around the corner!

"Ow! You're stepping on my toe," Chad whispered. "Can't you move forward a little?!"

Had the merc seen them? Heard them? Honestly, how could he not?! If the stakes weren't so high, Robin would have thought he was a part of a cheesy comedy.

As if on cue, the elevator doors let out the loudest groan and began opening. Finally!

But the doors didn't open normally, side to side. They opened vertically, like a mouth yawning. And ever so slowly! It was agony. Clearly, someone needed to grease the piece of junk!

Anika reached out. The closest to the elevator, she pushed on the doors to open them faster.

That's when the gunfire erupted.

BRAPP, BRAAPP!

The statue's head exploded! Dust and marble rained down around them.

The elevator doors creaked open wider . . . wider.

"We're going to have to take off our backpacks," Anika yelled. "Otherwise we'll never fit!" Slipping her own off, Anika didn't hesitate. With the opening just big enough, she dove inside. After tucking into a roll, she reappeared and began yanking on Chad's arm. Despite his smaller size, he didn't seem to fit.

"Ouch! Stop, stop! You're going to pull my arm off!"

BRAPP, BRAAPP!

The statue's arm, severed at the shoulder, fell. When it hit the floor, it shattered into a million pieces. More marble dust and debris rained down, coating Robin. He continued to huddle down further and further behind the shrinking statue.

BRAPP! BRAAPP!

Apparently, Chad hadn't understood the art of turning sideways. Because as soon as he did, he was gone. Sucked into the elevator.

There was little remaining for Robin to hide behind. The statue had to look like one of those classic armless, headless statues from history books. Yet the elevator doors *still* hadn't opened up fully.

And now it was difficult to see. The dust was blinding Robin. He could hear the mercs approaching. Their footsteps were closer. Louder!

So, grabbing the first bag his hands came to, Robin—

BRAPP, BRAAPP!

Clenched his eyes shut—

And dove for the gap!

Had he made it? Robin couldn't tell until he rolled over and stared up at the elevator ceiling.

Bullet holes punched through the back of the elevator.

But now the outside doors wouldn't close. Anika leaned into them, lifting the bottom door for all she was worth.

Robin jumped to his feet. Wiping the white marble dust from his eyes the best he could, he yanked down on the upper door.

P-TING, P-TING!

The metal on the elevator door bubbled inward from the gunfire. The doors approached each other an inch at a time. The narrow band of light from the hallway continued to shrink.

Until the strip of light disappeared—both sets of doors fully sealed shut!

The elevator lurched upward. It groaned and creaked, carrying its new cargo.

Robin and Anika slid to the ground, exhausted. In the glare of a single overhead light, they rested with their backs against the door.

Robin looked down. Covered in white powder, he nearly resembled a statue himself. He reached for his backpack, but it wasn't there. None of the backpacks had made it into the elevator. Then what had he grabbed? Anika's duffel bag lay beside him. Drat, they had lost nearly all their gear!

Robin felt around his cargo pants, pulling out the McDonald's bag. Phew, at least they still had the diamond.

That's when Chad stepped out from the shadows of the elevator. "You guys do realize that as I'm the safecracker, you really don't want me getting hurt. I mean, maybe it's time that Sneaky, Inc. ponies up and pays to have my arms and hands insured. Then, I would help more."

40

The elevator rumbled upward.

BZZZZzzzZZZzzZZ!

The elevator suddenly made a new noise. By the sound of it, the buzzer announcing the approaching floors was dying. Or maybe it was already dead.

The first floor marker blinked on.

For once, the doors had little difficulty opening. That was a relief. Robin wanted to get his team out of there as fast as possible. There was no way the kill squad could have found another way upstairs as fast as they did. Not that the elevator was all that fast. But still.

Robin stepped out. And immediately stopped. Several couples dressed in their formal attire, apparently laughing at a joke, greeted him. Their laughter stopped as they all turned toward Robin.

Awkward.

Stretching out behind the couples was the entire gala. A live jazz band played fast melodies from another era. While some guests danced, others sat at the little round tables covered with silk tablecloths dotting the floor. Servers presented bright red lobsters along with champagne flutes balanced atop silver trays. Festivity was in the air. Robin looked down at his own clothing: a smudged black outfit, latex gloves, and a loaded duffel, with a fine dusting of white marble overlaying all of it. Robin looked like a criminal.

Before any of the guests could say anything, Robin stepped back into the elevator. His finger jabbed at the button labeled 2. Robin didn't quite know what else to do. He offered a smile and a little wave. The doors finally closed and the elevator groaned back to life.

"What are we going to do now?" Anika asked. "There's only three floors total, not counting the basement."

"We'll get off at the second floor." Robin jabbed at the button again, trying to coax the elevator along. "Doesn't this bucket of bolts go any faster?!"

"How are we going to exit from the second floor?" Chad asked.

"I don't know!" Robin said, frustration building. He studied the control panel, looking for the Go Faster button. "I'm making this up as we go, Chad. You got any better ideas?!"

"Not really, but I can recommend the exhibit on the third floor." Chad pulled out his phone, holding up a photo. "They've got a cool samurai display."

At the end of his patience, Robin pressed his head against the wall. He tilted it just enough to see Chad's photo.

There was a moment of heavy silence.

"You are *not* serious."

"Remember that place where we went and got dressed up like cowboys, and they took our photo and made us look all old-fashioned? They need to do that with this exhibit, seriously! If they are having any problems selling general admission tickets, I can promise you this would get things moving again."

"Chad, can I recommend you return to the world where people are shooting at us?! And why are they doing that? I don't know. Maybe it's because we just happen to be carrying a diamond worth more money than any of us will ever earn in our lifetime." Robin paused for dramatic effect. "Combined!"

Robin thrust forward the mangled McDonald's bag.

Chad drew in a long breath through his nose. "Oh, doesn't that just make you hungry? I mean, I can practically tell what that bag had in it before."

Robin shook his head, opening his mouth for a response.

And that's just when the electricity went out.

The elevator ground to a standstill.

Plunging them into darkness!

41

"THEY'VE CUT THE POWER," Anika said, cracking a light stick and shaking it. The pale green glow illuminated their faces.

Shoving his glasses up on his nose better, Chad pointed up toward something. "And we're stuck between floors." An ancient numbering system above the door displayed their dilemma.

Robin took in a deep breath. He began pacing. His head tilted back. He whispered a prayer. "Lord, please give us wisdom without finding fault. Because we need it now. Actually, let me rephrase that. Please give us wisdom, *especially* without finding fault. The emphasis being my own."

"We're like fish in a barrel, sitting here. They're gonna hit us from above."

Robin reached out for the glow stick. "Can I borrow that?"

Anika handed it over.

Robin looked up again, studying the ceiling. Aiming, he tossed the glow stick upward. The ceiling was high up, at least ten feet. But sure enough, the light revealed something. Robin threw the light stick again. There it was again: the faint outline of an emergency hatch.

"Alright, we're going to climb out of here. I want to get above them before *they* get above *us*. Let's move!" Robin cupped his hands together. He hoisted Anika into the air.

With one hand on the wall, Anika stepped up higher onto Robin's shoulders. It was a wobbly tower, but it would have to do.

"It's locked. We could try to pick it or just dissemble the whole thing."

Robin groaned. "Whatever's faster!"

"Chad, dig through my duffel bag. Find the cordless screwdriver and the security bit set."

"Roger that."

ZIIPPPP!

Chad unzipped her bag and began digging through it. "Whoa! You have so much junk in here, do you know that?"

"It's the one with the yellow handle."

"Oh, I didn't know you brought along our skateboards. Is that what was digging into my side earlier?" Chad asked, holding up the proper tool at last.

Anika immediately got to work on the hatch screws.

BRRIP, PING! BRRIP, PING!

With each turn of her screwdriver, a new bolt fell, bouncing on the floor.

Chad eyed his skateboard. "I'm assuming this would be a bad time to practice my kick-flips."

"YES!" was the response he got in unison.

"Fine, fine. I was merely asking."

"Okay, last screw." *BRRIP, PING!* Anika handed down the heavy door plate.

"Chad," Robin said, his voice shaking. "You're the first up."

The boy didn't hesitate. Chad scrambled up Robin and Anika like a monkey on a tree. For Chad's little size, the kid certainly was nimble, Robin had to give him that.

But they were running out of time. Precious little time before the mercs were back. Likely in even more force!

Atop the elevator, Chad reached down, helping Anika up through the hole.

It was a relief to Robin as her feet lifted off of his aching shoulders. He watched as she completely disappeared into the hole above.

Her face quickly returned. "Toss up my bag."

Zipping it up, Robin began swinging it. At just the right moment, he let go. A perfect throw.

Anika caught it on the first try and pulled it up and away.

Robin had a sinking feeling beginning to creep over him. With their backpacks abandoned, that meant all their rope was gone.

He didn't want to think about it . . . until Chad's and Anika's faces suddenly appeared again. His friends looked so high above him. So far away. Even when Robin lifted his arm, it felt like he was miles below where they were.

"What . . . what about me?"

42

From her perch above, Anika yelled down to Robin. "I dug through my duffel but I don't have anything to help us. I'm sorry, Robin." He looked far, far below her. "We'll find something, I'm sure of it. Trust me! We'll be right back."

Anika scrambled away. She didn't want to see his reaction. She wasn't sure she could handle it. Anika approached the side of the maintenance elevator and looked down the crack between the elevator and the wall. It looked tight. She worked her way around the top of the elevator until she discovered a set of steel rungs built into the elevator shaft. Anika tilted her head back. It was hard to see, but it looked like Chad was already well above her. The only light in the elevator shaft came from cracks at each floor stop.

Anika climbed. She needed to find something long enough to reach down to Robin. Something she could tie off and that he could climb. But what exactly? It wasn't like she was at the mall. Or the hardware store.

The steel rungs felt cold and rough on her hands. A layer of dirt and dust had collected on them.

Anika didn't like this—leaving Robin. She would never leave a teammate behind. Not unless it meant rescuing them later.

But what if Ledger's men arrived before she did?

Anika climbed faster.

The light started to get brighter. Chad must have figured out how the doors worked. Anika looked up and watched as he pressed a lever, manually overriding the second floor doors. Light from the hall now crept in.

Anika climbed the last few rungs. It was a big step from the ladder to the gallery floor. But Anika leaped it easily.

An exhibit featuring World War I spread out before Anika and Chad. There was a haunting lineup of gas masks, spiky helmets, and barbed wire on display. Even through the dim light, Anika could make out the depressing brown and gray colors of the exhibit.

Anika crept forward. She tiptoed through the display. But nothing looked like it would help Robin. Nothing was long and climbable.

Maybe this had been a mistake. Stealing the diamond. Maybe Anika should have put her foot down and told Robin it was unwise. Unsafe!

At least, he claimed that the final decision had been up to her.

Or was that only a lie?

Antiquated cannons. Vicious clubs with pointy spikes on the end. Deactivated landmines for tanks. All horrible, horrible ways to die.

Anika turned away.

Nothing here would work—rats! She couldn't lower any of this . . . this junk! And why did a museum keep such a terrible display? Being surrounded by death and destruction was only adding to her stress.

A new thought. What about the next gallery over? Maybe they had something useful. Did she have time to go look? And how far away was it? What if they only had paintings? Or worse, sculptures?!

Out of the corner of her eye, Anika suddenly caught movement.

She signaled to Chad. Both of them knelt, ducking behind a display of amputation saws.

Three shadowy figures approached. The silhouettes of their rifles easily gave them away.

Ledger's killers!

43

Isabella stood outside of Starbucks.

She didn't want to sit down. She didn't want this to take any longer than it needed to. Everything she was doing right now felt stupid. Stupid—and exhilarating at the same time!

If this worked out as planned, the group wouldn't even know about it. And they didn't need to know, honestly. It would just be her little secret.

So, why was Isabella feeling so jumpy? The mocha she had earlier didn't have that much caffeine in it. But her foot tapped relentlessly on the sidewalk.

She looked at her watch.

Maybe she should just go back to the trailer. What if Robin called while she was out? Okay, she had her earpiece with her. That wouldn't be the problem. But what if he wanted the research results on the guests? She could always say that she needed to use a restroom. And unless they wanted to buy her a larger trailer with a bathroom inside of it . . .

A car drove closer. Was this her delivery?

The car continued on.

Maybe Isabella should run into the Starbucks and use the restroom. That way, if someone asked, she would be telling the truth.

But if she left this spot, she might miss the Uber. Ugh, this wasn't supposed to be complicated. Any minute, the driver would meet her out front, on the sidewalk.

Okay, fine. Maybe getting a delivery in front of a Starbucks was weird. Isabella didn't care. She'd never see the driver again. She could just be herself.

What Isabella wanted right now was a little grace. But giving grace to yourself sorta felt odd.

Isbella clamped her hand on her leg, forcing it to stop twitching.

This was all wrong. She shouldn't be out here. Isabella decided to return to the trailer. Going into the gala was completely overboard. Too much! Just a passing fancy that she should have ignored.

Isabella practically leaped from her spot to cross the road.

Only she forgot to look both ways.

HOOOONNKK!

The car's brakes screeched!

Isabella stood frozen in the headlights of the approaching vehicle. Stillness. Silence.

The bumper had stopped an inch away from Isabella's legs.

She was shaking. Where had the car come from? She never even saw anything. Maybe she had been too caught up in her own thoughts to see it actually—

"Hey!" the driver of the car yelled. "Don't you know how to cross the street?!"

Isabella didn't know what to say. She was so flustered. And what made it even worse was that she recognized the voice. Where had she heard it before? And why was she having so many issues with voices recently?

The driver's door opened.

For a moment, the person remained a silhouette. The headlights were too bright for Isabella to see.

"Oh, I don't believe this," the driver said, stepping out of the car.

Isabella shielded her eyes and took a step back toward the sidewalk.

No.

Yes.

It was Brad. He was wearing a new T-shirt that read: "Uber driver. Because handsome isn't a job title."

And if that wasn't bad enough, Brad stood there holding Isabella's long white box.

"You again?!" Brad grumbled. "Is this some sort of joke? Are you seriously trying to send me to prison?!"

44

ROBIN PACED.

There wasn't anything else to do. Not when you're trapped in a large, rusty freight elevator without power.

Anika's light stick continued to glow where it lay on the floor.

Robin tapped on his earpiece again. "Izzy, you there? Come in, come in."

Silence.

"Anika. Chad. Anyone?!"

No response.

Maybe the elevator was blocking the signal.

Or maybe not.

Robin wanted to punch something. He didn't enjoy waiting. And when exactly were his teammates coming back? How hard was it *really* to find a rope or something?!

It had only been a few minutes, but it felt like an eternity.

Robin didn't like doing nothing. He scooped up the glow stick and began tossing it and catching it again. At least it gave him something to do.

He paused, looking back up at the open hatch.

Way too far. He had already tried to jump it, but that was a joke. He wasn't even close.

Robin paced again.

The kill squad would have all the equipment they needed when they arrived. Like shooting fish in a barrel. Any minute they would swoop down on him. He would hear them when they came, repelling down the elevator shaft. And then what? Robin didn't think Ledger was the sort that took prisoners. One shot to the head and Robin would no longer be a threat. It didn't matter that he was a kid. One shot was the simplest solution.

Robin paced faster. Why didn't he ask Chad for a vapor torch? He could have cut a hole in the floor.

Robin stopped pacing. And then what? The first floor of the museum was extra tall. Thirty feet maybe. Then there was the basement. It had high ceilings as well. The fall from the elevator would be at least sixty or seventy feet to the bottom.

That was a loooong way down.

Why did this operation have to involve great heights? All of them recently?! Why couldn't the FBI give him a job on the ground for once? On sweet, solid earth!

No more. He wouldn't take it. If the FBI came to him with even one more job that involved anything taller than five feet, he wouldn't do it. No, siree! The FBI could find someone else to do their dirty work above that height.

Robin looked up at the empty hole above him.

Did he hear a noise?

Anika said they would be back, right? Robin didn't misunderstand her . . . did he? They wouldn't just leave him down there, would they? Stuck in a pit, left to rot.

The haunting thoughts washed over Robin. He didn't know what to believe anymore. He didn't know what was true and what wasn't.

To stop himself from screaming, Robin bit his lip. Or was it to stop any tears?

"God, what is taking them so long?!"

More silence.

"Why is it that you don't answer me when I need you to, huh?!" Robin growled. It felt good to talk. To vent what he was feeling. And it made him believe he wasn't alone.

"Why don't you just fix all of this? Just snap your fingers and make it all go away. Or is that asking too much?" Robin cringed as he said the last part. He knew that was wrong. Like trying to poke a finger in God's eye. That really wasn't what he wanted.

Only, Robin felt angry!

Angry at his teammates. Angry at Ledger. Angry at God.

And although he wouldn't admit it, maybe most of all—

Robin felt angry with himself.

45

CHAD CREPT OVER BESIDE Anika.

"There's going to be more of them soon," he whispered. "I've got an idea. I'll draw them away while you get Robin out."

Anika scowled at Chad. "You aren't going to set the museum on fire or something, are you?"

With their rifles strapped to their backs, the three mercs began unloading bags of gear beside the open elevator doors. Large coils of rope emerged from duffel bags. Rappelling harnesses, clips.

Anika leaned in close. "What do you need?"

Chad smiled.

A simple smile is supposed to put people at ease, isn't it? Yet Anika did *not* feel good about Chad's grin. Whatever that boy was cooking up surely meant trouble.

But then again, what choice did they have?

If they didn't do something quick, Robin was done for.

Chad quietly unzipped Anika's duffel bag. Fishing around, Chad appeared to know exactly what he wanted.

Apparently, he only wanted one thing.

His skateboard!

"Brad, how in the world would I know you drive for Uber? I assumed your hands were full with Brad's Amazing Ender of the World Printing Service!" Isabella barked. This time, saying his company name didn't feel embarrassing. Was she already jaded?

"Are you and your friends videotaping me? Right now? Is it going to go up on YouTube or something? Because if this is one of those channels where you put people in awkward situations just to make them squirm, so help me—"

"It's not, Brad. I promise you! Can I just have the dress?"

Brad hesitated. "I should probably make you sign an NDA before I hand this over, you know?"

Why was he so hard on her?! This felt crazy!

Grace. *Grace.* Isabella relaxed her neck muscles.

"Brad, no. We don't need an NDA. I'm sorry. I'm running late, so I really can't stay here and work out all the legal ramifications of my simply taking the dress from you—the one that I bought with regular U.S. currency. Will you give me a second chance, huh?"

Brad shrugged. "Okay, fine. Just promise me one thing, will you?"

"Yes, Brad. I'll promise almost anything."

"Promise that you'll write to me when I get sent to prison. Will you?"

Isabella blinked.

Brad kindly handed over the box.

Isabella practically ripped it out of his hands. And tucking it under one arm, she ran!

Over her shoulder, she yelled, "I will, Brad. I promise. I'll write!"

🏛

I want you to be a truth teller.

Robin stopped in his tracks. Should he drop to his knees?

"Yes, I'm sorry, Jesus. Please forgive me for what I said earlier. I was just—you know—being a jerk."

Speaking what is true makes your words real. Something others can rely on, hold on to.

Robin opened his mouth, but then thought better of it. He still didn't see why this was such a big deal, but maybe he should just listen. Maybe Robin needed to sit with what he had just heard.

Do you know what that hole does?

That hole? Excuse me. Was this still the whisper of God? What hole? Robin's immediate thought was that the "hole" was a metaphor for sin. Like what sin did to his relationship with Jesus. It made a hole or a rip in it.

But Robin had been staring at something while he thought. Something right in front of him, and he hadn't realized it. It was like he had zoned out.

His eyes suddenly focused on a tiny hole in the elevator door.

It wasn't a bullet hole. The manufacturers had built it into the door on purpose.

Wait a minute. Wasn't that an emergency door release? Didn't you need a skinny pole or something to poke inside of it? Didn't that release it?

Hope resurged inside Robin!

But he didn't have a skinny pole! He didn't have anything like that. All Robin had was a bunch of nothing and—

A light stick.

A long, skinny light stick!

46

CHAD POPPED UP LIKE a gopher. Springing onto his board, he kicked forward at a mad rate.

Weaving between displays, Chad tipped over the poles strung with red velvet cords keeping visitors back.

One after another the stanchions fell.

BLANG, BLANG, BLANG!

Ledger's mercs spun. Their ropes and equipment lay abandoned. Rifles swung up on their shoulders.

KR-BLAM, BLAM!

Anika flinched as the World War I display came to life, glass and gas masks jumping about. How could Chad remain so calm? Didn't he realize they were shooting at him?!

KR-BLAM, BLAM, BLAM!

Chad slalomed the gallery room and exited.

Two of the guards immediately ran in pursuit, reloading their clips.

Only one merc remained. After looking around, he went back to his work with the ropes beside the open elevator shaft.

This one would be Anika's focus.

Keeping low, Anika crept closer to the remains of a shattered display. As slow as a glacier, she reached up, threading her hand through the broken glass.

Her hand felt each item, eventually finding its mark.

Anika quietly pulled down a wooden club that bore a set of horrible spikes at the end.

Inside the trailer, Isabella checked the radio controls.

Had she missed any messages? There was no way of knowing.

No. Surely she hadn't missed anything.

With a smile, she turned to the long box on the floor. This was so exciting! Isabella hadn't had a beautiful dress like this in years. She eagerly tugged at the ribbons holding the box closed.

Isabella hesitated.

Why did this still feel like a bad idea? If she was going to rethink walking into the gala, now was the time. After she pulled off the box top, there was no going back, she knew that much. Once her eyes saw the crimson silk, she would be smitten. All arguments to abort her plan would be gone.

Isabella glanced at her computer screens.

Everything was working fine without her. She wasn't really needed anymore. Her job that evening was done, right?

Isabella attacked the box like it was Christmas morning.

She gasped. Isabella had been right.

The dress inside was simply stunning.

Maybe even better than she had imagined.

Irresistible!

Robin threaded the light stick into the hole. It fit perfectly.

KR-CLICK.

It was quiet, but Robin could feel the pressure from a latch as it released. And just as he yanked out the light stick, the inner set of doors gently slid ajar. Without much effort, he pushed them fully open.

A bare concrete wall faced him.

Great. How was that going to help?

Robin stepped closer to the edge of the elevator. There was a gap, but not much of one.

He looked down. Into the deep, dark, inky blackness below—

And shuddered!

Robin's stomach filled with acid. His hands shook. *Don't look down. Don't look down.* He forced his eyes away, choosing to look upward.

The dim light from the open doors above was just enough to see by.

Could he fit inside this gap?

Chad certainly could have, but could Robin? He wasn't sure.

And there was nothing to hold on to. No handrails here in the narrow space. He'd have to shimmy his way up, pushing between the wall and the elevator, keeping a constant pressure between them.

Would that work?

47

THIS WAS THE PROPER way to appreciate a museum.

On skateboard!

Chad continued to thread his way through different exhibits and from one room to the next. Occasionally, he even had to slow down just to make sure his two pursuers hadn't gotten lost.

Chad tooled past oil-painted landscapes.

Some had sheep grazing on the grass. Others displayed people lounging on the greenery in fine clothes.

KR-BLAMM, BLAMM!

Okay, that one didn't have people lounging anymore. It had several large holes instead. Modern art?

Chad kicked forward again, gaining speed. He didn't want to get sloppy. After all, these guys behind him clearly didn't appreciate fine art as much as Chad did.

And then he spied something.

Up ahead, a new display greeted Chad. He couldn't help but grin. He didn't slow down. Instead, he held out one hand as he zoomed past.

Chad examined his plunder.

It looked sorta like a remote control for a TV. Only this was *way* better and *far* more interesting!

Chad glanced behind him. The two guards had finished reloading and were aiming again.

KR-BLAMM, BLAMM, BLAMM!

But none of what was behind him interested Chad anymore. What he held in his hands was the new thing! A number printed on the wall flashed by. Chad poked the number into his remote and then held the wand up to his ear.

His audio tour began: "The nineteenth century was a golden period for landscape painting, both domestically in America and abroad."

Isabella's dress fit like a dream!

She smoothed her hands again over the folds of silk down the front. Honestly, she could *not* have asked for better sizing. Now if only there were a full-length mirror in the trailer.

Isbella slipped on the heels from the bottom of the box. Yes, she had spent far too much money! But honestly, how could she buy such a stunning dress and *not* get the right shoes to go with it? It felt like it would have been a crime to cut corners.

Isabella flopped into the chair and spun around to the computer monitors.

A small display showed the visitor report had finished. She air-dropped it to her phone. There wasn't enough time to go through it. There would be time for all of that later.

Right now, there were more important things.

Isabella double-clicked on the Zoom icon. Then she flipped open the plastic guard covering the webcam.

Using her own video feed like a mirror, Isabella began applying lipstick.

Anika wavered. She couldn't actually hit someone with this dreadful mace, could she? It felt so barbaric. So terrible!

But then again, wasn't that what her job called for? When a teammate's life was in danger.

Anika crept forward again. Maybe she should go back to using her blackjack. It worked nicely on Robin earlier. The incident was unfortunate, but it had proved to be a good testing ground.

Rats! She didn't have the blackjack anymore. It was in her backpack, abandoned in the basement.

Anika paused to watch the remaining merc.

K-THUNK, K-THUNK!

The guard installed explosive bolts into the wall beside the elevator opening. Then he clipped several carabiners onto the bolt ends.

Anika dried her hands on her pants. She started forward, then stopped again.

What was she thinking?! The merc wore a kevlar helmet and body armor. Her club wasn't going to work. It wouldn't do anything! She was going to have to find something else. Something that could—

That's when the guard spun around.

He looked ready to descend into the elevator shaft.

Except their eyes met.

48

Robin inched himself upward. He clenched the light stick between his teeth.

He had successfully stepped out of the elevator and wedged himself in between the car and the outer wall.

It was a tight fit, which didn't give him much room to apply friction. But so far so good. Robin was actually making progress.

And good progress at that. He only had—what?—about five more feet until he'd be at the top of the elevator. From there he should be able to climb up and join the others.

The others. They were alright, weren't they? Why hadn't they come back? Did they just forget about him?

Robin grunted and shimmied up another inch or two. He had to fight the negative thoughts. He knew his friends were faithful. They must have run into trouble.

Robin's muscles burned. They needed more oxygen, but when he went to take in a bigger breath, the light stick slipped out of his mouth.

He wanted desperately to reach out for it, but he couldn't. Not without losing his grip.

Robin watched as the pale green light tumbled below.

It lit up the walls as it passed them, like a car driving through a tunnel.

It seemed to fall forever . . .

Before it bounced several times, finally resting on the bottom.

The light was only a pinprick below him.

Far, far below.

Robin swallowed hard and focused his attention back upward.

He gave another push.

Chad hopped off his skateboard, kicking it up into his hand.

He glanced behind him down a long, grand hallway. The mercs were back there, a good distance behind, and they looked winded. Were they on their walkie-talkies?

Chad had bigger problems. He gazed forward again.

A giant set of escalators sloped down before him. They weren't running. Someone had likely shut them off to keep the gala attendees from using them.

And Chad only had one shot at this. There was no chance at a redo. He couldn't just run back up the escalator to try again. So, it had to be done right the first time!

Hmm. Chad studied the wide center area between the escalators. Ride down it like a surfboard, or face first like a snow sled?

He glanced behind him again.

One guard had taken a knee. Hold on. Was that guy using a scope?

P-TING, CRASSHHH!

A glass panel beside Chad exploded.

Oooh, or he could always sit on the skateboard and ride it down the steps. That could be fun. But then again—

P-TING, SMASHHH!

Chad sheltered his head from the glass erupting around him.

A grin spread across his face. Yes! He knew what he would do. He pulled out his phone and positioned it high above him, into selfie mode, when—

P-TING, POP!

A bullet hole punched clean through his phone.

Chad's jaw dropped. He put a finger through the hole just to make sure it was really there. His grin faded.

"Hey, you JERKS!" Chad yelled, flinging his phone as hard as he could down the hall at the guards. It fluttered about but didn't get anywhere close to his target. "I WAS USING THAT!"

"Aww, forget it," Chad sulked to himself. He climbed up onto the center part of the escalator and, flopping down, simply slid down on his butt.

49

THE GUARD IN FRONT of Anika dropped his rappel rope. He scrambled for his SCAR rifle slung over his back.

Anika leaped forward. Her club swung through the air.

It was perfect timing. The mace met the barrel of the rifle.

CLANG!

Metal on metal! But Anika's club didn't stop there. It ricocheted, slicing through the front rifle strap.

K-BLAMM!

A shot went off, going wide. The merc fumbled the weapon. He didn't have time to get a good grip on it. And now, without the strap, the rifle dipped forward, slipped through his fingers.

It spun in the air and took a nasty hit on the ground, finally coming to a rest between them. An easy reach for either one of them.

But the merc didn't lose a beat, swinging a fist.

Anika arced backward, the guard's knuckles only inches from her face.

She recovered, choosing to focus on the rifle. If the guard got ahold of it again, it would end the fight. And her.

As the guard recoiled from the missed punch, Anika kicked at the weapon. It wasn't a great kick. Her foot only connected with the edge of the gun.

Yet the rifle spun away, skittering toward the elevator opening. It stopped short of falling in, hanging halfway over the edge.

Seriously? It couldn't have gone one more inch!

Anika dodged three more jabs.

She would have to get behind the merc now, somehow. A simple kick would rid them of the rifle for good. But how could she get there?

Anika swung the spiked club again. At best, it was a half-hearted swing. The guard easily dodged it. Anika simply couldn't bear to hit him with it.

The guard offered an evil grin. He must have realized his advantage. And it looked like he was willing to use it.

Anika didn't see it coming. A swift kick with his steel-tipped boots. It knocked the mace out of her hand and sent it halfway across the gallery.

Anika took a step backward, reeling, trying to find her balance.

But she should have looked where she was stepping. Her foot slipped on a piece of glass.

Anika felt the ground moving before she slammed onto the gallery floor. Her hand slicing open on the shard of glass.

That was all the time the merc needed. Without rushing, he turned around and calmly grabbed his rifle, rescuing it from the ledge.

Anika scrambled backward, crab crawling, desperate to find safety. But there was nowhere to hide.

The only possible weapon within reach was a tiny shovel that lay beside her. A spade for digging trenches.

Anika immediately grabbed it and threw it. It didn't even come close to hitting the guard. Instead, it soared wide and clattered down the elevator shaft.

Anika felt all hope drain out of her.

The guard aimed the rifle at Anika. His finger slithered over the trigger.

This wasn't how Anika had imagined it would end. One never does. She had hoped to grow up, get married, have kids—grandkids?—and die at a ripe old age. Maybe in her sleep, yes. But not here. Not like this. And definitely not by the hands of a terrorist. By someone who had no problem shooting a child. An unarmed one at that. By someone with such dead eyes.

His finger squeezed.

CLICK!

For a fraction of a second, the guard looked up, catching her eye. One filled with horror, the other with surprise. The rifle had misfired. Malfunctioned. Because of the nasty drop it had on the ground?

It didn't matter.

The merc took a step back, desperately trying to fix the rifle jam.

And that's when Anika noticed his foot. He had stepped into a coil of rope. His own rappelling rope.

Anika lunged forward. Ignoring the pain in her hand and the blood, she grabbed the end of the rope. With everything she had, Anika pulled. Jerking the rope hard and fast!

The rope went taut, catching the guard's foot. With his focus elsewhere, he teetered, losing his footing.

A hand shot out to steady himself. Only the wall was too far away. He took another step . . .

Only there was no more floor behind him.

He screamed—

As the elevator shaft swallowed him whole!

50

THUDDD!

Robin heard the crash. Something had landed right above his head. Were they throwing things at him now? Then he heard the gunshot. Now it sounded like they were tossing statues!

A few inches more, and Robin would be at the top of the elevator.

But that's when he hit it. A slippery patch!

Thick and goopy, it had to be axle grease. His hands had nothing to cling to. Robin slipped.

NO! The drop below was unforgiving!

Robin thrust his other hand upward.

And to his surprise, there was actually something there. Robin grabbed it and clung to it with his life! With a fresh surge of adrenaline, he hauled himself upward.

How did a steel-toed boot end up here on top of the elevator car?

Robin climbed higher, using the boot as support.

But why was a guard there? One of Ledger's kill squad?

Finally on top of the elevator, Robin rolled over and lay on his back, exhausted. The guard's chest continued to rise and fall. His little trip must have knocked him unconscious.

Anika's head suddenly appeared in the opening above.

Robin offered a little wave. "Hi."

"Hi."

"This gentleman with you?" Robin nodded toward the body.

"Briefly," Anika said, pulling something out of her hand that glittered in the light. "He wasn't really my type so, well . . . I had to dump him."

"Bad joke." Robin coughed, wiping his hands off on the merc's sleeve. "Very bad. Remind me never to date you."

Minutes later, Robin and Anika sat in a darkened stairwell, wrapping their wounds.

Both of them were too tired and too hurt to talk.

Robin gingerly stood. His muscles ached all over. He needed to push himself to finish the job. After all, they weren't out yet.

Robin approached a set of doors labeled: First Floor. Did he dare try them? He gently opened one door. No alarms went off. That was good news. Isabella's software override worked just like she said it would.

Everything was working in their favor again.

From his cargo pants, Robin pulled out the McDonald's bag. It was still there, snug and well protected. He couldn't help but unwind it for another glance.

Just a quick one.

The Star of Flame Diamond glistened back at him. It really was amazing. A priceless gem, lost to centuries of treasure hunters, now rested in a McDonald's bag. In the hands of a fourteen-year-old.

His fourteen-year-old hands!

Robin wrapped up the diamond again, shoving it down deep into a pocket. Okay, so they got distracted a little and had to take a detour. Not a big deal.

Their exit was close. Almost within sight.

Only one hallway and two doors, and they would be free—out of the building. From studying the map, the doors looked only twenty feet apart. The museum clearly had them positioned apart for security reasons. Except Isabella had solved all of that. Security was no longer an issue.

Yet being this close didn't give Robin permission to be careless. If anything, it meant that the team had to focus all the more. Mistakes could still be made.

But it was hard *not* to get excited.

Just a little!

"It looks clear," Anika whispered.

"You ever imagine wearing a diamond this big?"

"Focus, Robin. We're not home yet."

"Yeah, I know, but could you see yourself wearing it to the school formal? Before we give it to the FBI, of course."

"No," Anika growled, her eyes focused on the hallway in front of her. But then she turned toward Robin. Her tone softened. "Well . . . maybe."

"Can you imagine what all the other kids would say? How they would react to seeing something like this around your neck? I mean, you'd be the center of *all* the talk."

Anika shook her head like she was freeing it of distraction. But Robin was only having a little fun. And he wasn't ready to let it go just yet.

"Or I could see if Isabella would want to wear it."

Anika's eyes narrowed. "You're that quick to pass it around, are you? Maybe I should have tossed you down the elevator shaft after all."

"Oh really?" Robin said, pushing past Anika. "Only if you can catch me!"

Scanning left and right, Robin raced ahead to the first door.

With his hand touching the crash bar, he paused. Robin shot back one of his lopsided smiles. His eyes were wild with fire and excitement!

But when he shoved the door open—

BEEEEPPP! BEEEEPPP!

Alarms blared!

51

Looking like a princess, Isabella had just stepped out the trailer door when the computer began beeping. She hesitated. Did she really want to know what that was?

Fine!

Isbella marched back into the tight trailer. She hoped that the cramped quarters wouldn't rumple her dress. At least no more than it already had!

It was the alarms. Someone had set off a museum alarm. Why didn't her software stop it? Coding could be so frustrating sometimes. You get a bug buried deep inside your code and try as you might, you can never find it.

Hunched over the computer, Isbella pulled up a few windows. Could she at least shut off the alarm? Her fingers danced over the keyboard without success. Had the security team already changed their own code?

It didn't matter.

Surely she would have heard from the others if there were a real problem. The alarm was likely a mistake. A person from the gala had opened the wrong door looking for a bathroom. That was all.

Probably.

Isabella clicked the window closed. She had better things to do than hunt down bugs in her coding.

A twinge of guilt. Maybe she should check in with the others.

Isbella gingerly held up the over-the-head microphone/speaker to one ear. She didn't want to mess up her hair. "Robin, Anika, come in."

Static.

"Chad? Can anyone hear me?"

Silence.

Was the museum using a signal jammer now? Everything had been working just fine before. Had something gotten triggered when they were in the bunker and killed cell reception?

Or was the team just busy? Maybe it was unrealistic to expect them to answer right away.

Isabella set her headset back down and slipped in one airpod.

Just in case.

Then with a dainty skip, Isabella exited the trailer.

52

Anika watched it all go down.

She hadn't chased after Robin. Something hadn't felt right. Off.

And it all happened so fast. Fast enough that Anika didn't know what to do.

With the alarms wailing, a steel barrier descended over the outer door. There was no way Robin could make it in time before the gate came down. It was too far away. Why couldn't he see that?! Why didn't he turn around and come back? They could go back up the stairs. They could find another exit!

Instead, Robin tried for the impossible. He sprinted for the last door.

"No! Stop!" Anika heard the words come out of her mouth. What good would they do?! How else could she stop him?

And if things weren't already bad enough—

Chad suddenly appeared. He flew in on his skateboard from a side hallway. Was he even watching where he was going? Apparently not.

Chad completely nailed Robin. It was an ugly hit. Both of them flew off their feet.

Ouch!

And if the hit on the marble flooring wasn't bad enough, Chad's skateboard added more. It rocketed into the side wall. Flipped into the air and returned. Onto Robin's head!

If he didn't have a concussion from her blackjack, he did now.

Anika only knew one thing right then. She could no longer help. Not as the armed guards surrounded the boys.

There had to be, what, six of them? Surrounding her friends.

Rifles pointed.

The last thing Anika saw before quietly closing the stairwell door—

Was the handcuffs.

53

ROBIN FELT A STREAK of something warm running down his cheek. Sweat?

Blood?

And Chad was beside him. Where had he come from? And why were they both sprawled out on the floor?

And rifles, inches from his face. Why? And was someone handcuffing Chad?

Robin couldn't exactly remember where he was and how things had turned upside down. He instinctively held up both of his hands. He didn't want any trouble. He just wanted the world to stop spinning. This had not been his day for head injuries. Maybe he needed to start wearing a helmet on these jobs.

Jobs. Wait, was he still working a job?

Yes, yes he was. Wasn't the exit door close by? All Robin could remember was that he had to get to the exit.

Robin fumbled to his feet and staggered toward the door.

Only, a giant metal barricade stood where he remembered the exit once being. Had they moved the exit?

And then someone struck Robin with the butt of their rifle.

And he didn't remember anything else.

Robin's eyes flickered open.

The world had stopped spinning, but man, he had one giant headache.

Wait. This had to be school. Was this chemistry? Because he wasn't sure if he had done the homework. And Robin knew he didn't bother studying for a pop quiz just in case—

Robin blinked a few more times. This wasn't chemistry. It looked like a storage room with large black crates around him. A large, square pillar occupied the middle of the room.

His memory returned sluggishly. The FBI. The tower crane. A diamond. The rifles.

The diamond!

Robin couldn't lose the diamond. He still had it, right? In his pocket? They didn't take it, did they?!

Robin tried to stand up. Only he couldn't. Was he actually tied to a chair? Who still did that?!

And who in the world was reciting chemistry facts?

"The atom is the basic unit of chemistry. It consists of a dense core called the atomic nucleus surrounded by a space occupied by an electron cloud. The nucleus is made up of positively charged—um— something or others, and—"

"Chad? Is that you?!"

"Yup." Chad's voice came from somewhere behind Robin. "I figured with all this free time, I should just do a little prep. You remember Mr. Brown said that we have a test on Friday, right?"

Robin groaned. "Are we alone?"

"For now."

"Do I still have my backpack? No, wait. We lost those at the elevator. What about the diamond? Is it safe?!"

"Um, what do you want first? The good news or the bad news."

"Chad! Just tell me!"

"Okay, the bad news is that yes, they took the diamond."

Robin slumped.

"From what I overheard, they already put it back. They also found the extra pair of underwear I hid in my socks. So, I'll be honest, that was a little embarrassing."

"Chad, I really don't care about your underwear."

"Oh, you would if they were a pair of Aquaman Underoos, trust me! It's not likely I'm *ever* going to see those babies again. Do you understand how hard they are to find these days?"

"Chad, the good news," Robin said, shaking his head and immediately regretting it. "What's the good news?"

"The good news is that I have a *killer* idea for a new business book. You wanna know the working title?"

"No, Chad. I really don't. I want to get out of here."

54

ROBIN DIDN'T HAVE MUCH to work with.

Except for the plastic crates surrounding the central pillar. And his massive headache.

Looking around, Robin couldn't see any supplies or tools within reach. No convenient knives or box cutters just laying around. Not surprising.

Robin examined himself. One arm was zip-tied to the arm of the chair, while his other arm had been bent behind him. He couldn't see it, but it felt like it had also been zip-tied. His legs wouldn't work. His ankles must have been lashed to the chair too.

Could Robin break the chair?

Robin wobbled up and down in the seat but got tired fast.

The chair looked to be at least eighty years old. Solid and made of metal.

He had really gotten beaten up this time. Robin needed a vacation. Or maybe just to have life return to normal for a while.

Why had Ledger's goons let them live? It would have been easy for the mercs to knock them off. Robin and Chad were only a liability. Why keep the two of them alive?

Okay, Robin could figure a way out. He just needed to be patient. And for his head to stop throbbing. Robin needed to focus on one step at a time. His leg muscles were the strongest. Robin began wrenching his leg back and forth. He didn't have much mobility. Robin tried moving his knees from side to side, bending and stretching the plastic bands around his ankles.

It wasn't doing anything. Was it worth continuing?

Robin worked his knee back and forth, harder, faster.

SNAP!

Sure, enough, the zip tie on his right ankle broke!

Yes! That was a start. Slow and steady wins the race.

Unless, of course, the guards returned.

No, Robin had to keep going. They had no chance with the mercs unless they were free.

Robin used his right foot to help put pressure on his left ankle. He pushed, using his other shoe for leverage.

SNAP!

It wasn't much progress, but now both of his legs were free. "Chad, you getting anywhere?"

"With the escape or the business book?"

"The escape, Chad. I'm sorry that was confusing."

"No."

"Try bending your knees side to side. You should be able to break the zip ties that way."

Robin had a little mobility in his hands since it was only his wrists that were lashed. He scooted his hips over to one side of the seat. Lifting his waist up off the chair, he managed to undo the magnetic clasp holding his belt together. Inch by inch, he worked the belt off his pants.

Pushing and probing, he managed to feed his belt under one wrist strap.

Gripping his belt with his teeth, Robin awkwardly reconnected the magnetic clasp. His belt now encircled the zip tie that bound his wrist. He let the belt loop fall.

Robin lifted a foot until it slipped into the belt loop. Pushing away, he added pressure to the belt until—

SNAP!

The zip tie broke! Now, Robin had two legs and one arm free. He jumped up from his seat, careful not to twist the arm bent behind him.

By now, Chad had gotten both of his feet free. He frantically wobbled an arm like a chicken wing.

Robin grabbed Chad's lashing and broke it. He couldn't believe their luck! Their escape was easier than he could have imagined.

Ecstatic, both boys were now on their feet. Only to find—

A shiny pair of handcuffs bound them together.

Robin stared at their newly discovered binding. "You have got to be kidding me!"

"What in the world?!" Chad cried as he tugged on the handcuff around his wrist.

"Hey, you can't *yank* on it without *yanking* on me!" Robin yelled, pulling his arm back.

"Ow! What are you doing? That hurts!"

"And it hurts *my* wrist when *YOU* go yanking on it!"

This was not going to work!

55

Robin liked Chad well enough. After all, they had been good friends since what—second grade? Little League?

But being chained to the boy was an entirely different matter.

And Robin had to get free!

Chad walked toward the storage room door, while Robin went to explore the crates. Neither one of them got very far.

"Don't you want to get out of here?!"

"Yes, but I want to cut these handcuffs off first!"

"What if there is a hacksaw sitting just outside the door?"

"What if there are bolt cutters sitting just inside one of these crates?!"

"Fine," Chad said, walking closer. "I can be the mature one."

"Oh, great. Yes, very mature," Robin said, pushing up on a heavy plastic lid. "I just want a peek, alright? It's probably more artwork."

Robin and Chad both looked inside at the same time.

But there was no artwork.

And no bolt cutters.

Only a stack of smaller wooden crates inside the plastic crates.

And it was the labeling on the wooden crates that was most disturbing.

C-4 plastic explosives.

Several control devices sat atop one of the open wooden crates. Sure enough, the entire thing was wired to explode!

"Well, you were right," Chad said calmly. "It ain't exactly bolt cutters, but it will certainly help us with our handcuffs. Wanna try it?"

Robin didn't answer. He couldn't. His brain was spinning at a thousand miles per second.

Explosives. This changed everything!

Why would Ledger spare the boys a bullet to the head, only to kill them with explosives?

No. This was far too much C-4 just for getting rid of a couple of meddlesome teenagers.

Robin eyed the three other plastic crates. He quickly unlatched them and flipped open each lid.

Sure enough, each crate mirrored the first.

Robin stepped back.

If Ledger wanted Robin and Chad dead, a quarter of a stick would have done it. This was far beyond overkill. This was enough explosives to take down the Sears Tower!

What was Ledger trying to do?

Robin stepped away—

Forgetting that Chad was still attached. "Hey, are we gonna do this all over again?" Chad yanked his arm back. "'Cause, trust me, I can play this game all day."

"No, I'm sorry. I need to think."

Robin wanted to pace. Like he always did when he needed to think, except now the handcuffs stopped him.

Think. *Think!*

"Lord, I know that you and I need to work out a few issues, but will you please give me wisdom right now? Without finding fault?"

Robin tilted his head back. His eyes followed the giant support pillar up to the ceiling twenty feet away.

The support pillar.

What was Ledger thinking, with that much explosive next to a support pillar?! Wasn't this one of the crucial beams that helped to hold up the museum? Didn't he know how dangerous that was?!

Unless . . .

Robin's face went white. Ledger was going to blow it up. The entire museum!

Puzzle pieces started to click together. That's why the workers were in a rush to remove the artwork in the basement. Those were probably the most expensive works. The ones that were irreplaceable. Ledger was no dummy. He wanted to save the best before he destroyed the rest of it!

But why? Why destroy it all?

Robin's head continued to ache. Nothing made sense.

Or did it?

"Why did Ledger throw the gala?" Robin asked out loud. "And why did he pull it together at the last minute? Like he was *desperate* to have it?"

"I thought it was because we robbed him. We took away the money he needed to put his terrorist plans into action."

"Precisely! Chad, will you do something for me?"

"I suppose. What?"

"I want you to pace with me, alright?"

Chad tried to keep up with Robin's manic pacing. But very quickly the turnarounds became an issue. The handcuffs forced them to adapt. Instead of going back and forth, they marched in a circle.

"So, Ledger needs money and fast, right?" Robin asked.

"Didn't we know that already? Isn't that why he's selling the diamond?"

"Yes, but this goes so much deeper," Robin said, suddenly stopping his march. "He's not really interested in selling the Star of Flame Diamond. He could have done that online, couldn't he? He might have raised twice the money." Robin began pacing again.

Chad struggled to keep pace with all the starting and stopping. "Don't forget, he charged a lot just for the entrance fee."

"That's peanuts, Chad. That's nothing compared to what Ledger's going after. Just think about it. Why would you want to blow up your own museum, huh?"

"Because he doesn't like modern art?"

"Insurance. That's where the real money is. What if Ledger took out a new policy?"

"Wouldn't the museum already have insurance?"

"Probably, but it wouldn't be hard to get more. Knowing Ledger, this would be a new policy specifically to protect against acts of terrorism."

"Oh, man. A terrorist taking out a policy against his own terrorism?" Chad asked as he tried to bite his nails on his cuffed hand.

"What kind of insurance money could Ledger get for a museum accident? With the death of a thousand gala attendees?"

Chad blinked. "But why would Ledger want to blow himself up? And his diamond?"

Robin grinned. "He wouldn't. All Ledger has to do is ride one of the tubes down into the basement. Along with his precious diamond, he'd escape in the bombproof bunker. Safe and sound!"

"Oh, wow. That guy really is rotten if he's willing to kill all his guests just for the money!"

Both boys stood still, trying to take it all in.

"Ledger plans to survive the explosion," Robin added. "And after a few days—maybe a week—simply walk out of the rubble. He could either go into hiding after that and pretend he's still dead, or—"

Robin hesitated. His voice became little more than a whisper.

"Or he could make himself a hero. The lone survivor of his own terrorism."

56

ANIKA SLIPPED THROUGH THE shadows.

Were the boys still alive? She could only hope.

Hope and pray.

"Dear God, please keep those two knuckleheads safe. And help me find them."

It wasn't much of a prayer, but it was all Anika could do. She hadn't been much of the praying sort. But ever since Robin and Chad invited her to youth group, prayer had somehow come to mind more often. It still felt weird to pray. Was she talking to some old man with a long beard? Did he sit on a big throne in an even bigger throne room? Empty and alone? Did he look down on the tiny humans and yawn?

It didn't matter. Her silent prayer probably bounced against the ceiling like a child's lost balloon.

Anika was on her own.

She could do this. Anika had to learn from Robin's mistake. You are never home and free *until* you are home and free! She wouldn't let such a disaster happen again. Not on her watch.

Anika crouched behind an empty desk. The smell of dust lay heavy on the air. The staff must rarely visit this area of the museum. It made sense to take the boys somewhere hard to find.

Anika had followed the guards the best she could. From a distance, she tracked them far enough to know that Robin and Chad were somewhere back in the endless basement.

And now, Anika traced them through the dust.

Footprints and streak marks. They must have dragged Robin when he was unconscious.

She had to be close now. Didn't she? The guards wouldn't have moved around aimlessly. Had they interrogated the boys? She didn't want to think about her friends being tortured. Anika pushed it out of her mind. She simply had to find them, whatever condition they were in.

The odd thing was how silent the basement had become.

The workers and the trucks had all vanished.

The crates that remained looked abandoned. Left in a hurry, just as they were.

And where were the guards? Earlier, the place had been crawling with them. Now the basement felt eerie. Like an abandoned ghost town.

Had Ledger sent them home for the night? Was their shift over?

Or was something much worse about to happen?

57

Isabella stood in shock.

Where had all the gala attendants gone? The front of the museum felt entirely too empty. Unguarded.

The gatekeepers were missing.

She had doctored up her own digital invitation and now there was no one to show it to. That felt odd. It seemed like the biggest party in town had suddenly been left to run on its own.

Isabella hesitated. She could still hear music playing and the sound of voices from inside. Her climb up the long front steps slowed. Had something happened?

She started having second thoughts.

Again!

No. Isabella was just feeling nervous. That was natural, wasn't it?

Maybe the attendants had stepped away for a moment. Maybe they were helping out elsewhere.

Yes, Isabella was sure that was it. It had to be.

She walked through the grand set of front doors. She smiled. Part of selling it is making it look like you belong.

The party inside was still underway. Couples danced, and from the looks on their faces, they were having the happiest time of their lives.

Isabella lifted her chin, holding her head up. She wasn't going to sneak into this party. Let them look at her. Let them take in her stunning dress! Isabella was happy to be seen. After all, she had been personally invited by this Mr. Smith *himself,* whoever he was. Isabella had the invitation on her phone to prove it!

She looked around. What Isabella wanted first was a drink. Fruit juice, if they had it. With her nerves on edge, her throat had gotten quite dry. A crystal glass of grape juice would really hit the spot!

Isabella began milling around.

But she couldn't find any servers. Did the guests pay ten thousand dollars just to serve themselves?

Isabella slumped down at an empty table. Somehow showing off her new dress hadn't been quite as thrilling as the idea of it. Most people were absorbed in themselves.

Something smelled good. Where was that coming from?

Glancing across the linen tablecloth, she saw several half-finished plates lay scattered. A few glasses sat empty, tipped on their sides. Where were the busboys? Did the waitstaff go home?!

More out of boredom, Isabella reached for her phone. Tapping a few apps, she pulled up the report that she had generated. Who were these people around her?

Who *exactly* had been invited to the gala?

58

ROBIN TRIED THE DOOR to the storage room.

Locked.

No surprise there. Should he try to kick it open? That felt a little risky. If there were guards, Robin didn't want them to know he and Chad had freed themselves.

But on the other hand, surely the guards had a way out. Or was Ledger planning to blow up the museum with his staff inside? Were they those kinds of terrorists? The ones who would give their lives for the cause?

That seemed crazy.

Could Robin do that? Did he believe in anything enough to die for it?

Maybe. Or at least Robin hoped he did. Weren't truth and justice worth giving up his life for? What the FBI fought for? Or had even the FBI lost their focus? The temptation to please others had a strong pull.

Truth and justice. Were they what this was all about? Sometimes Robin couldn't remember exactly. Sometimes the diamonds got too bright and shiny.

"Dear Jesus, guide us to do what is right," Robin whispered. "To do what *you* want us to do. Even if it costs us." Robin didn't like those last words. He really hoped it wouldn't come to that. Giving up his life, or any of his friends' lives, felt bigger than he could handle. "And grant us all the courage to do what you ask of us."

"I see a vent up there." Chad pointed. "It's pretty high up. But we might be able to reach it if we move some of these crates."

Robin looked for himself. The vent seemed small. Like, claustrophobic small. He frowned. He had no interest in trying to squeeze through something that tight. Maybe Chad could do it, but not Robin.

What other options did they have? Robin continued to search the walls. Nothing. The guards had locked them into an impenetrable storage room made of concrete. It would take nothing short of the explosives to free them.

Other than a miracle of course.

"Dear Jesus," Robin prayed again. He said it loud enough that Chad could hear. "Could you help to get us out of here? Maybe just open our prison door, like you did for Paul and Silas?"

Anika followed the streaks in the dust along the floor.

The trail led to a closed door up ahead.

But where were the mercs? They wouldn't just leave the boys in there alone, would they? Was this a trap?!

Anika hunched over, listening. She didn't hear anything. No sounds from people in hiding. The only sounds she heard were from water moving through the pipes overhead.

How long should she wait?

How long until she knew it was safe?

The idea of praying came to her again. But she wouldn't give in to it. Praying was goofy, wasn't it? Like writing a letter to Santa with your wish list.

Anika brushed a tight curl of hair away from her eyes.

She had no idea what lay on the other side of the door. Or who. There was simply no way of knowing without any of her tools.

This was madness!

"God, if you exist," Anika whispered, surprising herself a little, "then please make this work."

Anika boldly stood up.

Taking a step forward, she made a fist and tightened it.

Step after step, she advanced. Quiet. Ready to swing at anything.

Only, she made it to the door without interruption. The door looked locked but—wait, was the key still in the lock?!

Could she just open it? What if the guards were behind the door?

Pressing an ear against the door, she listened. Was that a voice? She couldn't quite tell with the noise from the water pipes.

Taking a deep breath, Anika twisted the doorknob.

Using her shoulder, she rammed open the door—

Her fists ready for action!

59

THE DOOR CRASHED OPEN!

As close as he was, Robin nearly got clipped.

He blinked.

A figure looking like an angry bear ready to attack stood before the boys.

"Anika?"

The angry bear softened.

"Robin? Chad?" Anika's fists dipped.

For a moment, everyone just stared at each other. Like a miracle or something had just happened.

Robin cleared his throat. He wanted to diminish the look of shock on his face. "Um, good timing."

Anika nodded, pushing away the unwanted emotions surging up inside her. "Yes, um, thank you. Are you guys alright?"

"Yeah, we're peachy keen," Chad offered. "They didn't do anything to us, other than take the diamond. I'll be honest, I was waiting for the torture to begin any second. I actually thought you were them when you opened the door. You guys have any tips on how to prepare to be waterboarded?"

"No, sorry," Robin said. "You mind if I take it from here?"

"Go for it."

Robin showed Anika the crates. Explaining his theory on Ledger's plan, he got Anika up to speed.

"So, you really think before Ledger sets off the explosives, he's going to escape into the bunker just like the diamond did?" Anika asked. "That's crazy."

"You tell me. You saw the bunker. He's gonna ride out the destruction in style."

"If the whole place is going up in smoke, no wonder the guards are gone. But what about the gala guests? There have to be hundreds of them. How do we get them out of here?"

Using hand soap and water, Isabella rinsed out someone's champagne glass at the bathroom sink. Filling the glass with water, she guzzled it down, surprised at how thirsty she was.

After filling it up again, she strolled around a nearby gallery. The overhead lights were off, but there was still plenty of exhibit lighting to see by.

Finding a long bench in the center of the gallery, Isabella sat in front of a painting titled *Lady Agnew of Lochnaw*. The painter was John Singer Sargent—nobody Isabella had ever heard of. Isabella could feel the intense gaze of the lady in the painting.

Pulling out her phone and sipping her "extravagant" drink, Isabella flipped through the spreadsheet data. What could she learn from that evening's guests?

The list was long. Too long. Too many names and too much data. She picked a few names at random.

They really weren't that interesting. Rich. People connected with the government. A few were officials. Others were people high up in different task forces. A handful were religious leaders. The people didn't look that interesting or exciting.

Isabella looked up at the lady in the painting. Whoever this Lady Agnew was reminded her of her own mother, a little. The long dark hair and pronounced eyebrows. Lady Agnew even had her same eye color. Why couldn't Isabella have gotten her mother's beautiful eyes, instead of dull gray? The exact and unusual eyes of her father?

A new thought: Maybe tonight's guests had more in common than just big bank accounts.

Acting the part, Isabella took another sip from her glass.

She searched the data for recurring words. Repeat phrases suddenly started popping up: "national security," "antiterrorist," and even "law enforcement."

Hold on. That didn't make sense. Why would a suspected terrorist be inviting this crowd to his party? It didn't sound like a list of friends. It almost sounded like a list of a terrorist's greatest enemies. That would mean—

"Hey," a voice interrupted. "Don't I know you?"

Isabella jumped to her feet, knocking over her water glass. But she couldn't have planned it any better. Her gown twirled. Isabella's long dark hair flipped just right!

Only—it was Chad. He was coming up through a basement door.

Oh no. Nonono. Chad simply couldn't catch her actually *inside* the museum! There was no way *he* could ever keep his mouth shut!

Ack! Too late.

Robin and Anika slipped in behind Chad. Were the boys holding something together? Were those handcuffs?!

But it was the looks on their faces that were priceless. Eyes wide. Mouths hung open in astonishment. It was exactly the reaction Isabella had been hoping for all along, by wearing such a gorgeous gown.

But somehow she knew—

It wouldn't last long.

60

Isabella looked amazing!

Of course, Robin wouldn't say that out loud. Heavens! Something like that could easily be misconstrued. Misunderstood. Blushing, he focused his eyes elsewhere.

And that's when he realized Isabella wasn't supposed to look amazing. No, wait. She wasn't even supposed to be inside the museum! What was she doing?!

His brow wrinkled. Robin open his mouth to complain, when—

Anika whacked him in the chest. She leaned in. "Compliment her first."

"I, ah, um . . ." Robin coughed, scratching one leg with the other. "I see you got a new dress."

"That wasn't a compliment," Anika growled.

"Yes it was!" he snapped back.

"What, this old thing?" Isabella said, spinning a full circle. She was clearly enjoying the attention. And maybe some of Robin's embarrassment too.

Robin planted his hands firmly on his hips. "Am I allowed to yell at her now?"

"No. We have to clear the building!" Anika said, taking charge.

"Why?" Isabella's smile disappeared. "What's happening?"

Robin stepped forward, forgetting he was still shackled to Chad. "Um, hello. Don't forget me."

Ignoring Chad, Robin went on to explain things to Isabella. They didn't have much time, so he gave her the short version of their discovery. Meantime, Anika ran off to the next gallery to find something.

Isabella took the news in stride. It was a lot to take in, and Robin didn't blame her for being shocked.

Just then, Anika reappeared.

With a scimitar.

"Listen, you two," Anika said, moving a small sculpture of a dancer off its pedestal. "This is the best thing I could find, alright?" Anika grabbed the boys' handcuffs and yanked them onto the cutting block. "We're just going to have to make do."

Anika heaved the barbaric sword above her head.

The situation finally registered with the boys.

"Wait just a minute!" Robin gasped, tugging his hand closer. "I don't know about this."

"Whoa!" Chad shrieked, pulling his hand from the center. "Have you done this before? Are you licensed with that thing?"

Anika sighed. "If you two can't keep still, then I'm going to chop off somebody's hand."

"Don't chop off mine!" Chad barked, starting another tug of war.

"Oh, so you're alright if she chops off mine? Is that what you're saying?!"

"How am I going to write my business books without my hand?"

"Seriously, that's your best argument? I'm surprised you didn't say, 'How am I going to pick my nose?'"

"Oh," Chad quieted himself. "I didn't think about that. Good point."

Anika frowned. She pointed to a statue behind Robin and Chad. "Now, what do you think he would say about all of this bickering?"

And just as both boys turned their heads—

The scimitar came swooping down!

61

K-CHINKK!

"AHH!" Robin and Chad both recoiled, flinching. But as they opened their eyes, they quickly found their own hands, thankfully, were still attached.

And better yet, Anika had severed the chain.

"Alright, that wasn't so bad." Robin pushed his handcuff further up his arm and rubbed his wrist. "Thank you for that, Anika."

She nodded.

"We're going to have to split up into teams," Robin continued. "Isabella and I will try to determine what controls the explosives. Our second goal will obviously be how to prevent the C-4 from detonating. Anika, you and Chad figure out a way to clear the building. I want all of the guests out of here, alright? I don't care how you do it. Any questions?"

Chad actually raised his hand. "Can I quote you on that?"

Robin hesitated. "Quote me on what, exactly?"

"The 'I don't care how you do it' part."

Robin's eyes narrowed. He spun toward Anika. "You're gonna have to keep him under control. Seriously, tell me if that's asking too much."

"I'll keep an eye on him."

"Hey, Anika and I are a perfect team," Chad said, giving Anika a side hug. "I'll keep an eye on her too!"

Robin's eyes narrowed even more. "I mean it, Anika. Keep that boy on a *short* leash."

"WHAT?! You're acting like I'm a kid. A kid in a candy store," Chad said with mock offense. A grin suddenly broke through. Chad began rubbing his hands together. "Okay, maybe I am, just a little. But wait until you see what I have in mind, muahahaha!"

Exasperated, Robin shook his head. "Whatever. Just make it work."

Chad raced off toward the stairs.

"The least you could do is wait for me!" Anika yelled after him. Turning the corner, they were gone.

Robin glanced at Isabella.

A silence hovered between them.

"Are you going to be able to work in that . . . that thing?" Robin asked, looking at her gown.

One of Isabella's eyebrows raised. "That *thing*?"

"You look lovely, by the way. Beautiful. I mean that."

"Thank you," Isabella whispered. She didn't know what else to say. Blushing, she spun away. "Alright, let's get to work!"

62

"JUST TELL ME YOUR idea, Chad," Anika said, taking the steps two at a time. Where was Chad going? He ran up the stairs like a fire had been lit underneath him.

"What? You don't like surprises?!"

"Alright, fine. Just let me in on a little of it, okay?"

Chad suddenly paused his manic ascension.

Anika clutched at the stitch in her side. She was glad for the breather.

Chad began tapping one foot. "Don't tell me you're the kind of kid who has to open up a corner of your gifts before Christmas. You know that's a serious offense, don't you? I mean, that's pretty close to a crime, if you ask me."

Anika opened her mouth, but nothing came out. There were *way* too many issues to address all at once.

"Okay, fine," Chad yelled, continuing his sprint upward. "I'll give you one hint! Galileo. There, I'm practically giving it away now!" Chad laughed, clearly pleased with himself.

Done with chasing him, Anika continued her slow and steady climb on her own.

Galileo?

That wasn't much of a hint.

Isabella led Robin back toward the great room and the ongoing noise of the party.

Robin clung to the edge of the festivities. He wanted to stay mostly unnoticed. His black thief outfit wasn't exactly a tuxedo. Especially after a night of being beaten up and things exploding. He'd cleaned himself up as best he could. But if anyone looked too closely at him, he would stick out.

The two slipped into an empty table near the back.

"What are we looking for?" Robin whispered, even though he didn't need to. The jazz band had just begun another song.

"It would likely be small and mobile," Isabella said. "That way he could keep it close to him. Keep control over it. It might look like a remote control of some sort. But it would likely have a keycode to operate it. He'd want tight security on it."

Robin nodded, fingering a bit of leftover icing on a plate.

"Why do boys do that?"

"Do what?" Robin asked, licking his finger.

"Eat that. You don't know where that's been. What if it was dropped on the floor? That's disgusting."

Robin laughed.

Isabella stifled her own laugh with a hand.

Not only did Isabella look amazing, she was funny too. Quirky and smart. For a moment, Robin wished that the party in front of them was just an ordinary, nonwork event. In a few short weeks, he and Isabella had become good friends. He could almost imagine inviting her to a nice dinner. One where they had to dress up and get all fancy. And maybe, just maybe, Robin would build up the courage to ask Isabella for a dance.

No. He would probably never do that.

How could he, when he didn't even have the courage to be vulnerable with her?

To confess that he had lied to her.

A figure suddenly approached the platform. He tapped on the microphone as the band finished their song.

From a distance, Robin couldn't see exactly who the figure was. Only that it was a tall man. Distinguished and wearing a tuxedo.

But from the first word out of the speaker's mouth, Robin knew him.

He knew the voice. All too well.

A voice that had continued to visit him at night, haunting his dreams. The voice from the walkie-talkie. A voice that sounded so sincere, so polite, and yet hid such a profound evil.

Robin shuddered at the simple sound of his voice.

"Welcome, everyone. I would like to kick off what may prove to be the most anticipated part of tonight's gathering: the auction for the Star of Flame Diamond!"

Only, to Robin's surprise—

Isabella went very still beside him. It almost looked like she recognized the voice as well. That, or she had seen a terrible vision. Isabella's face lost all color. Was she alright? Was she going to be sick?

Her hand suddenly lashed out. She grabbed Robin's hand.

What was happening? Robin didn't understand. As brief as it was, they were just laughing, having a good time a moment ago. Weren't they?

Something was wrong. This wasn't affection. Isabella's hand felt cold and clammy. Robin's thumb slipped onto her wrist. Her heartbeat hammered away.

"That's . . . that's Marlin Ledger," Isabella gasped. She was breathing too fast. If she didn't slow it down, she was going to hyperventilate.

"Robin, do you know who that is?" Her voice was now little more than a whisper.

Her pupils dilated, growing quite large. She wasn't going to lose it, was she?

"That's my father!"

63

THE WORLD ENDED.

That's what it felt like.

Right there, with the two of them nestled at the small bistro table. Amid a plate of half-eaten Black Russian cake and gold-foiled confetti littering the floor.

The truth of Isabella's words echoed between them. Robin couldn't quite understand. He had heard what Isabella said, loud and clear, but the meaning hadn't fully sunk in. It was too much.

The atmosphere between them changed. The air got thinner. It felt hard to breathe, and the weight of his surroundings hung heavy on him.

Robin's new finger of icing never finished its journey. It was frozen. Lost between table and mouth.

"I don't—I don't understand," Robin managed to whisper. "This guy couldn't possibly be your—"

A close-up image of Ledger flickered onto the large screens as the guests applauded.

Those gray eyes. As beautiful as a rainy day. Robin gazed into Isabella's face. He could hardly believe their resemblance. A mirror image of father and daughter.

"I'm sorry," Robin whispered. "I'm so, so sorry."

Isabella sat back, closing her eyes. Had he lost her?

Maybe this revelation changed everything. Was she even still on the team?

Isabella's lips moved. Robin couldn't hear her over the ongoing applause.

He leaned in.

Closer.

"We have to stop him," Isabella whispered. "He doesn't know what he's doing." Her voice gained volume and power. Her gray eyes opened. "I can talk to him. He'll listen to me. I can convince my father to stop. I know I can. I just know it!"

Robin wiped his finger clean on the tablecloth. "I don't . . . I don't think that's a good idea. Isabella, you have to understand. He has the entire museum wired to blow any minute! He won't be able to hear you. Not anymore. The wheels are already turning. It's too late. Too many things are already in motion!"

"No. I can do it. He'll listen to me. I can bring him back!"

Marlin Ledger stepped back from the podium. A tall lady dressed in black satin, her hair beautifully positioned atop her head, stepped forward. With a voice as silky as her dress, she began the auction.

"Isabella, we're running out of time," Robin said. "We'll be lucky if we have five minutes."

Isabella jerked her arm away like it had been burned. "You have to give me a chance. That's all I want. A second chance! Robin, he's my *father*."

Robin looked around. The bidding had begun, calm and polite like the fine-art auction it was masquerading as. The giant TV displayed numbers that continued to grow.

Forty-five.

Forty-nine.

What were these? Dollars?

No, they were millions! Robin blinked in disbelief as the numbers continued to leapfrog the previous bid.

Sixty-eight million.

Seventy-two million.

"Alright, Isabella. If the opportunity presents itself, I'll give you a chance," Robin said. He wasn't sure if he meant the words that he had just said. It all felt too risky, with too much at stake. "But let me talk to him first."

"You?"

"Yes! Remember, we have to find that trigger. We can't let him activate it. At least not before we clear the building."

Isabella stayed silent. Her piercing eyes drilled into his.

Was she angry? Maybe it was sorrow. It felt too difficult to tell.

"Trust me," he whispered as he suddenly stood up.

Robin never should have lied to her.

64

ROBIN MARCHED PAST THE restrooms.

He picked up the pace, jogging. Pushing open doors, Robin quickly found the kitchen area.

It sat empty. Abandoned.

Food lay in various stages of preparation. A nice slab of raw meat, half cut. Potatoes peeled, beginning to brown. Several pots boiled, unattended. Where had everyone gone?

There was no time. Robin raced through the columns of steam, looking for something.

Was this going to work? Or was this suicide?

Everything felt foolish now. Robin had no faith left that he could even pull off something like what he had planned.

The giant screen now displayed the number one hundred and twenty-seven point five. It continued to tick upward, but much slower now.

Robin tugged at his crisp, white sleeves. The jacket wasn't a great fit. His option with the formal servers' outfits ranged from too tight to way too big. The bow tie had been the biggest challenge, but fortunately he found one already tied. His black vest fit better than the pants.

None of this mattered, did it? The waitstaff was practically invisible. No one would pay attention to him.

Robin held a silver platter a little higher. As he walked forward, he snagged food bowls from several nearby tables and added them to the tray.

He approached the steps leading up onto the stage. He didn't hesitate. Robin had to play the part and not second-guess things. If he didn't look like he fit in or knew what he was doing, it would show.

And that could cost him.

Him and everyone else around him.

Robin swallowed. He boldly approached the first person at the side of the stage.

The gentleman wore a tuxedo, but it bulged outward on the right side. Robin glimpsed the ammo clip where it poked out of his coat. Robin diverted his eyes. He didn't want to draw attention to the fact he had noticed it.

Should he say something? His mouth felt dry. Instead, the guard selected a bit of caviar from off of Robin's tray and ate it. Not even once did the guard look at Robin.

Robin turned to serve the other guests who were on the stage. He positioned himself for service, always keeping Ledger in the corner of his eye.

Ledger was the last in line.

Chad and Anika stood before a ghostlike figure.

It was a bust of a Roman Caesar, made of pure white marble.

Anika finally erupted. "What are we looking at?!"

Chad held up one finger to wait.

And what was the long remote-control thing pressed up against his ear? Was he actually listening to something?

"Chad, we don't have time for this!"

"To answer your question, this is Emperor Domitian. Did you know he was another Caesar who was sadly assassinated by—"

Anika snatched the audio tour from Chad and tossed it across the room. "Good enough. We're taking this one?" Anika asked, pointing to the bust.

"Whoa, I was having an educational moment there. And I just want you to know, that was *at least* a twenty-dollar rental that you so kindly discarded. I hope you feel good about that. Granted, I did get it at a pretty good discount, so it's not like it was a complete waste."

Anika wasn't listening. She had already shoved past the velvet ropes and now bear-hugged Emperor Donutian, or whatever his stupid name was.

The statue was heavy. Stunningly heavy!

Anika groaned, barely able to inch the statue up off its pedestal.

Arching her back, she clutched it with both hands. "Aw, gosh. . . . Wanna help?"

"You're doing great, Anika. You've got this! Keep it going. You're looking good!"

"I didn't mean be an encouragement! I meant help me carry this thing!"

"Oh, yes, sorry," Chad said, gripping the side of the statue. "You want me to take back all the encouraging things I just said?"

65

Robin stepped up beside Ledger.

He held out his tray carefully, hoping to avoid eye contact.

Ledger turned and, after a quick glance, grabbed the closest champagne flute and sipped from it.

Now what?

Somehow, being this close to a known killer gave Robin the willies. A cold sweat ran down his spine.

So where was the trigger? And did Robin dare try to pick the man's pockets? On stage?!

What should he do? He couldn't just walk away . . .

"Beautiful party you have here," Robin said, looking out over the guests, trying to sound natural.

Ledger glanced at Robin again.

"I believe the waitstaff was instructed not to interact with the guests," came the cold response.

"Oh, I'm sorry. I was hired at the last minute. I must have missed that training," Robin offered with a smile.

Ledger's eyes narrowed. He turned just enough to look Robin over—head to foot.

Robin didn't move. He just kept smiling. And wondered when Chad's plan to clear the gala would begin.

"Do I know you?" Ledger asked, finishing his drink. He set the glass back down on Robin's tray with a hard clink. "For some reason, your voice sounds familiar. I don't believe we've spoken before, have we?"

Robin felt like melting.

His whole body wanted to cave in on itself.

To shrink until it was nothing.

Anika and Chad limped and struggled with the marble bust until—

THUNK!

They set it down on the edge of the balcony.

Anika couldn't feel her arms anymore. They were numb. Dead.

Shrouded in darkness in the top-floor gallery, Anika watched the auction continue far below.

How was this going to work? Chad still wouldn't explain anything. Was she doing the wrong thing by going along with him? What if his plan was pure madness?

"Wanna know something Galileo invented?" Chad asked. He untied the closest end of a long banner that stretched out over the gala room. It was one of many decorative banners draped high above the party. "Galileo is usually remembered for discovering the sun being at the center of our galaxy. You know, not the earth. But did you know that he also discovered the pendulum?"

Anika honestly couldn't care any less. She wanted to go home and fall into her bed. But she also wanted to live. And she wanted all the unsuspecting people below her to live.

So, Anika kept her mouth closed. Maybe if she didn't interrupt, Chad would get on with it.

She watched as Chad calmly carried the free end of the banner closer. Again and again, Chad wrapped the banner around the bust's neck before tying it off.

"You see, the invention of the pendulum is a pretty underrated thing. I mean, it isn't to science geeks like me, but you know, not everyone has that appreciation like I do."

Chad rotated the marble bust, carefully adjusting it.

Was he aiming it? At what?!

Chad edged the statue, firmly connected to the long banner, closer to the edge of the balcony.

66

"Me?" Robin said, clearing his throat. "I must have one of those voices that sounds like everyone else."

With a glance up at the big screens, Ledger slipped one hand into his coat pocket.

"Going once. Going twice." The lady in the black dress suddenly cracked her gavel on the podium. "Sold! At the price of one hundred and thirty-one million dollars."

The entire crowd exploded in cheers!

The applause and celebration was thunderous.

Robin watched as Ledger pulled out—

His phone!

Ledger's thumb hovered just above the lock button.

Of course! What better trigger than a phone! After all, phones were nearly impossible to hack into. And they could be customized to control the lift into the bunker below as well as trigger the explosives!

Robin gazed into Ledger's gray eyes. Familiar but so cold.

"If you recognize my voice," Robin said with a new boldness, "I hope you recognize it as a friend and not as an *adversary*!"

A lightbulb suddenly clicked on behind Ledger's eyes. Recognition!

Time slowed.

In complete shock, Ledger spun toward Robin, just as—

Robin snagged the stem of Ledger's empty glass, letting the silver platter and all its contents clatter to the floor.

"I'll need this too," Robin said and grabbed Ledger's phone!

With one finger, Chad pushed on Domitian's forehead.

The heavy marble bust suddenly disappeared, falling from the edge!

Anika gasped.

She watched on in horror as the banner swung away, threading between the aircraft connected to the rooftop. By the time she could actually see the Caesar again, the bust was hurtling above the guests' heads!

Aiming straight toward the tall and cylindrical—

Fish tank!

KR-CRANGGG!

It bounced off the side of the gigantic tank with a sound that commanded everyone's attention. All celebration suddenly halted. And as everyone spun around, they had the chance to witness a series of white spiderwebs rippling through the thick glass.

So, by the time the marble bust returned for a second strike—

SMASSHHHHHHH!!

They watched as half a million gallons of water erupted outward.

Right toward the crowd!

Isabella watched the wall of water as it approached, sweeping guests off their feet.

The water plowed over tables and the loudspeakers towering on stands. Sparks erupted, but just as quickly the water snuffed them out!

Getting ahold of herself, Isabella sprang to her feet and pushed her way through a nearby door. Using her back, she did her best to shove the door closed.

Only water already swirled around her feet.

Yanking off her heels, Isabella paused to catch her breath. Where was she? A utility hallway? Where did it lead?

Isabella didn't know. All she knew was that she had to get out of there and head upward.

The water continued to rise!

She had to find Robin, and more importantly—

She had to find her father!

67

ROBIN RAN TO THE edge of the stage.

The rising water gave him pause. Going forward wasn't an option. Robin only had seconds. And that's when he turned and spied it. A glass elevator towered above him.

He didn't have time to study it. But it stood above the water, open and waiting. Robin raced toward it, clutching Ledger's phone and drinking glass. Cries and screams erupted from the crowd behind him.

Robin entered the elevator, jabbing at the topmost button. He didn't really care where it went. He only wanted to get away from Ledger. As far away as possible!

As the doors began to close, Robin stepped back deeper into the elevator. He finally took in the magnitude of Chad and Anika's plan. Water surged over the Egyptian displays, washing away the mummies and knocking over guests like a rogue wave at the beach.

Robin also spied Ledger collecting his few remaining guards. Together, they made for Robin's elevator door.

Robin repeatedly stabbed the Close Doors button.

The clear elevator doors slid shut—

Just in time!

Ledger's mercs banged on the glass as Robin rose up into the air. With no time to lose, he dropped to his knees. Clutching Ledger's phone, Robin activated it.

The phone screen lit up. But sure enough, Robin couldn't get in. It wouldn't unlock. The phone asked for a thumbprint activation.

Robin held Ledger's champagne glass up, spinning it in the light. There! Ledger's fingerprints.

Would this even work? Robin had no idea. He gingerly placed the drinking glass against the phone and rolled the fingerprint over the scanner.

Denied.

No! Why didn't it work?

Robin tried again, this time rolling the drinking glass in the other direction.

Denied.

Maybe the fingerprint was only a partial. Robin held the glass up to the light again.

Finding a new print, Robin tried again and again.

Denied. Denied.

The glass elevator continued to climb. Frustrated, Robin noticed the giant aircraft overhead approaching.

Robin tried the phone once more before—*DING!*

For a moment, Robin thought he had done it. That the phone had unlocked!

But the noise hadn't been from the phone unlocking. It was from the elevator. Robin had arrived at the upper floor.

The elevator doors opened.

Robin checked the phone: `Unlocking is disabled for 1 minute.`

NO! That couldn't be! Robin *had* to get the phone to work. He had to get into it. Or what if he simply destroyed it? Jumped on it, or threw it into the water below?

Would that work? Or had Ledger's men programmed a fail-safe to trigger upon the phone's destruction?

Robin couldn't risk it. He had to wait and try to unlock the phone again.

Impatient, Robin scanned his surroundings. Where was he?

He stood on a round observation deck. It sat nestled in the center of the mighty aircraft display. A place where guests could witness history up close.

But Robin wasn't interested in history.

He needed a way out! And the observation deck only had one exit: the elevator.

That's when the elevator doors behind him began to close.

Robin reached out to catch them—

But he was too late. The doors closed in his face.

He watched as the elevator began to lower. Robin stepped back. It wouldn't be long before Ledger and the elites from his kill squad would arrive.

And now Robin had no place to go.

He was trapped!

68

ROBIN PEERED OVER THE railing.

His stomach clenched. Heights *again*! It was a long way down. Much too far for Robin to jump.

Robin reached for his backpack.

But it was gone. Rats! Robin didn't have anything now. He felt helpless without his tools. All he had was a useless drinking glass and a phone he couldn't unlock.

It felt like a complete waste of time, but Robin prayed once more.

"Jesus, please help me understand what I should do. Help me unlock this phone so that I can prevent the explosion."

Robin heard the elevator engines stop.

Through the glass, he watched as the giant gears reversed direction.

Ledger was coming!

Robin activated the stolen phone again. Should he try something different?!

Denied.

But this time there was a new additional message: `You have 2 more attempts.`

What?! No! How could this be?!

Robin wanted to throw the phone, but he didn't dare. He was out of options.

The elevator gears continued to grind.

The kill squad had to be close.

Robin caught his own reflection in the B-29. He looked like he was going to throw up. His face written in fear!

I want you to fly.

He heard the whisper, but it didn't mean anything to him. Did God want him to jump?!

And that's when his eyes followed along the giant aircraft. To the wing.

No. Nonono. He couldn't jump out onto that, could he?

It looked too far. No, it *was* too far! Robin couldn't do it. He didn't like heights. Trying something like that was entirely out of the question. Anika could do it, but not Robin. Jumping that far was simply foolish and would likely only end in a horrible fall to the—

DING!

Robin knew that sound.

Out of the corner of his eye, he saw the elevator doors begin to open.

So, ramming the glass and phone into his vest pockets, he ran.

Straight for the edge of the balcony.

He launched himself over the guardrail, using a bench to gain height.

And Robin flew!

69

THE AIRCRAFT WING WAS too far away.

Yet Robin hit the front edge of it with his gut! Above him, the metal groaned.

His hands clawed at the smooth, shiny surface. Robin couldn't get a good grip. He felt like he was sliding backward.

And by now the elevator doors had to be fully open.

Robin strained for one last reach.

He couldn't explain it in the moment, but it almost felt like he had been helped. Like a hand reached out and grabbed his, helping to pull. Maybe it had been a handhold built into the wing. Robin wasn't sure. He was only glad it was there!

Scrambling onto his feet, Robin sprinted along the top of the wing toward the body of the B-29.

BLAMM, BLAMM!

Bullets punched through the metal wing inches behind him.

Hanging only by steel cables, the aircraft began to sway. The sound of metal straining and rubbing echoed.

Robin used both arms to keep his balance. A hatch in the wing approached.

BLAMM, BLAMM, BLAMM!

Shrapnel flew around him. Gaping holes opened up beside him. Without hesitation, Robin yanked open the hatch and dropped inside.

By the looks of it, he was inside the area that once held the giant engines. It was hollow. Had the engines been removed to lighten the weight?

Robin scouted around, finding another door of sorts. He pulled it open.

On his hands and knees, Robin worked his way through a tight repair tunnel in the wing until it opened up. Robin stepped out into the main body of the plane. The aircraft was truly cavernous and stretched out in both directions. Had the engineers gutted this part of the plane as well? The museum's roof must not have been as strong as it appeared.

Robin looked forward and aft. Where to now? He really had no idea.

Robin pushed forward, opening an oval door in the bulkhead.

This was the cockpit where the pilots sat. From the unique window pattern, it reminded Robin of the *Millennium Falcon*. That brought a grin to his face.

He only wished the plane would stop swaying. The movement made Robin feel seasick.

At a dead end, Robin backtracked and explored the rear half of the plane.

Except for a few side doors, the aircraft was mostly empty. Someone had even welded shut the bomb bay doors.

Did he dare work his way out onto the other wing? But where would he go from there?

Robin nearly lost his footing as the plane suddenly rocked hard to one side. Had someone jumped aboard? From the grinding sound of the ceiling bolts, the museum roof didn't like the added weight.

Robin knelt. He had to try the phone at least one more time.

He positioned the drinking glass another way. Maybe the fingerprints needed to be displayed in a different orientation.

Denied.

`You have 1 last attempt.`

And that's when the plane jerked again. Robin lost his balance. The champagne glass slipped from his fingers.

SMASH!

"No!" Robin cried. He reached out for the broken pieces. But there were too many. Too small.

Robin sat back. Nothing had worked out right. Not like it was supposed to! Now Ledger would be on top of him. And Robin had no hope of unlocking the phone!

The repair hatch in the other wing suddenly swung open.

Chad's head poked through. He was grinning ear to ear.

"When I saw you jump out onto that wing, I just knew I had to do that too," Chad said as he climbed in. "I'm gonna tell you, I have *not* had that much fun in a *long* time!"

"I'm sorry, Robin." Anika followed behind Chad. "I tried, I did. But it was like telling a kid he can't play on the playground when it's right in front of him."

Robin stood, holding out Ledger's phone.

Anika took it.

"I don't know what to do anymore," Robin lamented. "I had his fingerprint, but I couldn't get it to work. I tried everything I could, but I've run out of options."

"Speaking of options, how'd you like the fish tank, huh?" Chad butted in. "The place is empty now. Everyone has cleared out."

Anika switched on the phone screen. She looked up at Robin. "One more chance? That's all we've got?"

Robin nodded.

Just as he felt a hard, cold piece of metal—

Press against the back of his head.

70

"I'LL TAKE THAT PHONE, if you don't mind," Ledger said.

Anika clutched the phone. Holding it to her chest, she stepped back.

"I'm asking kindly," Ledger said calmly, cocking back the hammer on the gun. "But I will have it."

Robin couldn't see behind himself completely. But his head turned enough to see that Ledger had lost his billionaire look. His tuxedo was now dirty, wet, and ripped in several places.

The ceiling rumbled and shook again.

Robin felt the plane tilt dramatically as two more heavily armed mercs dropped in from the back. Apparently, there was a ceiling hatch Robin had overlooked.

Even though Ledger's voice sounded controlled, there was a new fire in his eyes. "I would like my phone *now*, please," he growled.

Robin could tell that Anika didn't know what she should do. She glanced at the phone in her hands. She looked up at Robin. Confusion and fear filled her face.

They were in a standoff. One where no one could win.

Chad suddenly appeared through the front bulkhead. "Hey, you guys know where they got the design for the *Millenium*—oh." Chad stopped, seeing the guests. He moved forward, clinging to Anika's side.

The aircraft now swung so much that it was hard for people to keep their balance.

"I'm sorry, but I do have a schedule to keep," Ledger snapped. "So, if you don't mind—" He pressed his gun against Robin's head hard, forcing Robin's head to bend downward.

Anika wavered. Her hand held out the phone.

"No, don't," Robin whispered. He knew that as soon as Ledger got his phone back, he wouldn't hesitate to kill them all.

And that's when it occurred to him. Robin didn't need to unlock the phone. Robin could have simply bricked it—locked the phone so that *no one* could unlock it! Not until it was factory reset, which would have erased it. It was all so simple. A simple press with the *wrong* finger, and it would be locked for good!

Robin wanted to tell Anika. To say something! His mouth opened. But what could he say? Nothing. Not with Ledger's gun firmly pressed into the back of his head!

Ledger reached for his phone.

Just as the museum ceiling groaned louder, and then—

PINGGG!

It sounded like gunfire. The sharp noise echoed through the airplane.

Everyone froze. They exchanged looks. It hadn't been the mercenaries behind Ledger. They looked as confused as everyone else.

PINGGG!

The sound came again from above.

The cables holding the aircraft to the rooftop—they were breaking!

And believe it or not, Chad actually grinned—

And jumped up and down!

71

PINGG, PINGG!

Like a kid on a trampoline, Chad jumped over and over. The aircraft began rocking and swaying even more. The support cables continued to snap.

"Stop it!" Ledger yelled, suddenly turning the gun toward Chad. "Stop it NOW!"

Robin seized the opportunity. His right elbow rose sharply, catching Ledger in the jaw! Marlin's head snapped back. The gun dropped.

PING, PINGGG!

The B-29 suddenly tilted dramatically, listing to one side. Everyone lost their footing. Bodies slammed into the side of the aircraft. The phone popped out of Anika's hand!

PING—PINGPINGPING—PINGGG!

The nose of the aircraft tipped down. Bodies and guns and a phone began sliding forward. It was chaos! Robin couldn't tell which way was up anymore as a pile of bodies smashed into each other!

PINGGG!

Then, just as the blob of humans began to untangle, they slid the other direction!

Ledger's phone skidded close to Robin. He reached for it, straining, but it flew past!

Robin could feel the hulking B-29 smash into neighboring planes. From the sounds of things, a domino effect had begun. Support cables all across the mighty ceiling were giving way. And as more and more wires broke, it put an unrelenting pressure on different parts of the roof. With this dramatic shift of weight, how much more could it take?

Just as Robin nearly stood—

Another body would slide past, knocking his feet out from under him.

Using the metal ribs of the aircraft as support, Robin scrambled toward the cockpit. Once he got free of the sliding bodies, Robin made good time.

PING, PINGGG!

The weight shifted—left, right, up!

Using everything he had, Robin forced himself through the bulkhead door. Using the pilot chairs as a ladder, Robin muscled his way into the front seat. He slipped half of the harness over his head and chest. Anything to keep him attached to the seat when—

GRROAANNNN!

The sound was like an approaching freight train. Deafening and all-consuming!

Through the front windows, Robin watched as a hole in the roof above him yawned open, tearing, ripping! From the center outward, the ceiling began to collapse under its own weight.

Robin felt his stomach leap into his throat.

The ceiling had released them. The aircraft was in a freefall.

Grabbing the flight yoke, Robin used all his muscles to—

Pull it toward him!

72

AT BEST, ROBIN HOPED for a controlled crash.

But there was less control, and a lot more crashing.

Glancing back, Robin watched as the tail of the B-29 was completely ripped off. Ledger's two guards tumbled out in the process.

The first wing broke off next, slicing through the remains of the giant fish tank.

The other wing ripped clean through upon hitting one of the museum's support beams.

Were Robin's efforts any help at all? He couldn't know. And with both wings gone, the flight yoke had become useless.

SMASSSHH!

The massive relic that had survived World War II punched through the mighty glass entrance of the museum. A wave of metal and debris led the way. The flightless remains skidded down the wide set of front steps, leaving a trail of sparks and rubble in their wake.

With its colossal momentum, the fuselage jumped the sidewalks. Like a bulldozer, the wingless aircraft continued into the parking lot. It plowed through Mercedes and BMWs without discretion, shoving everything aside like they were Matchbox cars. Faroff car alarms blared while other closer vehicles were completely obliterated in the onslaught.

Clawing and scraping, the remains of the B-29 spun around until—

The behemoth finally ground to a halt, tilted to one side.

From what remained of the front windows, Robin had a front-row view. He sat, gasping for breath in the brief moment of stillness, as—

The Museum of Arts and Culture continued to cave in on itself! A mighty pillar of smoke and dust rose into the air.

As the roar of destruction settled, Robin slipped off the harness. He reached up and felt the cut on his forehead. The blood was running down into his eyes, making it difficult to see. Every muscle in Robin's body screamed out in pain. Man, would he be sore tomorrow! And was that *another* hit on the head? His concussion surely had a concussion now.

Robin stared at the remains of the museum.

Hold on. Where was he again?

Noises from behind him drew his attention.

Robin stumbled to the opening in the bulkhead. Weren't his friends supposed to be with him?

He gazed through the remains of the aircraft, over the spread of car parts, and across a shimmer of broken glass.

Chad stumbled out from behind the bulkhead door. "Now, I'm gonna tell you this straight. I would not be in a rush to do that again.

Not anytime soon, at least. I'd give it maybe a six out of ten. Super fun until the throwing up starts," he said, wiping his mouth.

A loose fender from a car suddenly moved. Anika shoved it aside and stood up. She was covered from head to toe in blood! "I'm alright. I'm alright!" She held up a ripped rescue packet of some sort. "It's not blood. It's only ink from a sea dye marker, in case the plane went down over water."

Robin sighed in relief.

And he saw it.

A cell phone.

It lay amid the rubble and loose wires.

Was Robin supposed to do something with a cell phone? He couldn't remember. His head was hurting more than he could ever remember.

The phone sported a nasty crack across its screen. But otherwise, it still looked intact.

Ledger's phone!

The memories rushed back all at once. The crane. The diamond. And the basement of explosives!

Robin dropped to his knees, reaching for the phone, when—

An expensive leather shoe stepped on his hand. The shoe was now scuffed and looked battleworn. Several of its laces were broken.

Robin lifted his eyes, squinting through the blood and sweat stinging them.

Ledger spoke. His voice was as rough and torn as his tuxedo. "It hardly seems necessary to blow up my own museum now, don't you think?" Ledger put more weight onto his foot, grinding Robin's hand into the broken glass littering the floor. Any more pressure and his fingers would snap. "Especially when the real terrorists have already destroyed it for me!" Ledger spat the last words like an accusation.

The pain was so intense! Robin could hardly see straight. He didn't know how much more he could take before passing out.

That's when Robin heard another voice. One that he recognized, although with so many hits to the head, he couldn't place it. It sounded quiet. It wasn't angry, exactly, but it did sound firm. Almost loving?

"Hello, Marlin. How long has it been?"

There was a pause. Robin blinked hard, but he still couldn't see the speaker.

The voice continued. "No, you don't need to turn around. And yes, that is a gun to the back of your head. Your gun."

Ledger let up the pressure on Robin's hand, but he didn't free him.

"You'll remember my voice, if you think back. If you really listen. Just one more voice that you discarded from your past life."

Robin suddenly recognized the speaker.

It was Isabella!

"I'm here now like a whisper in your head, offering you a wake-up call. A second chance. I'm offering you grace! If you let these three go."

"There is NO WAY I will ever let them—" Ledger's voice suddenly stopped.

What was happening?! Robin felt the pain in his hand relenting, being removed. But he couldn't see anything anymore between the blood and the pounding in his head.

How much time passed?

He didn't know.

His world was fading.

He was losing consciousness.

All he could remember was the feeling of someone lifting him by his arms.

Just before Robin passed out.

73

ROBIN'S EYES FLICKERED OPEN.

There were bright lights and machinery with all sorts of cables beeping around him.

A hospital?

Chad, Anika, and Isabella stood by him on one side of the bed.

A lady in her mid-forties, with brown hair that had begun graying on the sides, stood on the other side of his bed. She wore an off-white sweater with a turtleneck. She clung to it like she was cold. A worried look grew over her face.

Did he know this person?

Oh, wait. He *did* know her!

"Hi, Mom," Robin managed to say.

Robin's mother simply shook her head.

Chad spoke up. "Oh, don't worry, Mrs. Ford. I've already chewed Robin out for not wearing his skateboard helmet. I mean, if it was up to me, we simply would *never* ride skateboards without wearing helmets. Haven't I always said that?" Chad looked at his friends for support.

Anika and Isabella hesitantly nodded.

Chad continued. "Mrs. Ford, I personally will see to it that Robin does not even get close to a skateboard or a half-pipe for the next month. You know what, while he heals from his concussion, maybe Robin and I can write a business book during that time, huh? I can't get your son to stop talking about his interest in writing. What do you say, Robin?"

Chad stared at his friend with a big grin.

Robin cleared his throat. "You don't have to lie, Chad. My mother knows. She doesn't *like* what we do, but she knows all about it and the costs involved." He looked back at his mom and offered a weak smile. "But still, uh . . . we probably have some explaining to do . . . don't we?"

74

Robin lowered himself into a chair positioned before a large wooden desk.

The entire group had gathered at their headquarters in the abandoned grocery store.

"How's your head feel?" Anika asked.

"Better," Robin offered, one hand shielding his eyes. "The lights still seem too bright sometimes, but otherwise I'm okay. Except for the headaches, I mean." Robin sat forward in his chair. He moved slowly, turning his attention to Isabella. "Hey, while we're all here, I wanted to apologize for something."

Isabella shook her head. "No apologies needed. We're all good."

"Well, no, I'm not. You might be right—we don't need apologies—but I do need to ask for forgiveness. I haven't been very honest recently. Actually, I've told each one of you lies, and I tried to justify it to myself. I made up reasons for why it was alright. But it wasn't right. It was wrong. I was wrong, and I want to ask each one of you to forgive me."

"I forgive you," Chad said.

"I forgive you," Anika said.

"Is that what we're doing now?" Isabella sat down on the edge of the desk. "Asking for forgiveness? That sounds heavy."

Robin grinned. "Yes, and I think I may need it the most from you. You're part of this team. I should have told you who our target really is, rather than keeping you in the dark."

Isabella blushed. "I don't like this, you know. Is this what Christians like to do? Sit around and forgive each other? This is *so* awkward."

Robin nodded.

"Okay, fine. Yes, I forgive you, Robin. But I do want you to know, I was pretty mad at you at the time for doing it," Isabella mumbled. She didn't look very happy. "So . . . I guess this means I have to ask you all for forgiveness now, right?"

"Only if you've done something wrong," Chad said. "And you want to get it off your chest."

Isbella reached into a pocket and pulled something out. She tossed it onto the desk.

It was the mangled remains of . . . something.

A lump of brown paper, smashed and wadded up.

"Okay, I'm not really sure how to do this, so give me a little grace. I want to ask forgiveness. Is that right? First, for abandoning my post at the monitors and sneaking into the gala. I guess I was just so tempted by all the finery, I couldn't resist. Which brings me to the second thing I need to ask forgiveness for. I saw this sticking out of my father's coat pocket there at the end, and I kinda sort of borrowed it."

Robin reached out and began to unwrap the object.

It looked like a fast-food takeout bag. From McDonald's?

The contents dropped out of the bag into Robin's hands.

The Star of Flame Diamond!

There were several gasps. And then laughter.

All Robin could do was squint and turn away his eyes. The diamond was *way* too bright!

"I know it was wrong, but I wanted to enjoy it for a little. I wasn't going to keep it," Isabella said a bit sheepishly. "I merely wanted to wear it around and see how it looked on me."

"Wait," Robin coughed. "You wore it around?!"

"Only in my bedroom, don't worry! Nobody in their right mind would wear that out in public."

"Okay," Chad interrupted. "I guess if we're all asking for forgiveness, then it's my turn." He heaved Anika's duffel bag up onto the table. "I snuck back later that night and did a little digging through the rubble."

Everyone watched as Robin slowly unzipped the bag. He looked inside. Then he leaned back, shaking his head. "I'm not . . . I'm not even going to ask," he said as he lifted out a—

Suit of samurai armor.

"You don't understand. I looked *so* good in it! I thought this could be our new Sneaky, Inc. uniform. Whatcha think?" he asked as he slipped on the Darth Vader–looking helmet.

The group laughed even more.

"My turn?" Anika asked. "I took this." From her pocket, she slipped out a phone. A spiderweb of cracks covered its screen.

Ledger's phone!

"I thought this still might come in handy," Anika said. "The way I see it, we succeeded in protecting all the guests at the gala. So that's a win. We got the Star of Flame Diamond, so Ledger won't be making any more money off of that. Another win. But as for the destruction of the museum?" Anika pulled out several sheets of printer paper and unfolded them. "Ledger has already submitted his claim for the three point two *billion* dollar insurance policy."

"Billion with a *b*?!" Robin exclaimed. "That's crazy!"

"Unfortunately, Ledger was right. We helped make his terrorist claim look even more convincing. If he actually gets that kind of insurance money—and it looks like he will—that will be a major setback for us and the FBI."

Silence.

Most of the group's joy had fizzled and gone.

Anika continued. "I grabbed this phone before the police showed up. If we can figure out a way into it, we'll have access to Ledger's different accounts and personal information. That might help us track where the insurance money is going."

Robin got up from his seat. Tilting his head back, he began pacing. Slower than usual, but he did it. "That might just work," he said.

He paused and turned back around. "Alright. If we're being honest with each other . . . what do you all say?"

"I'm in," Anika said.

"Me too!" Chad said, having climbed fully into the much-too-big samurai suit.

Robin turned to Isabella. "And how about you? I want to respect your feelings on this since it is, well . . . your father we're going after. I honestly don't know what I would do if it was my own dad."

Isabella dragged a finger across the desk. "You know, you guys have already given me something I didn't deserve." She cracked a grin. "A chance to be part of *this* group—*this* family. I don't want to lose that. I am *convinced* my father will eventually see the errors of his ways. And that I can help him do it. But until then . . . count me in!"

Stay tuned for Sneaky, Inc. Book 3: ***Operation Meteor!***

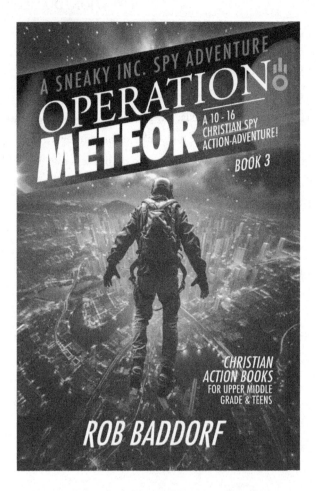

Continue the adventure with
OPERATION METEOR!

Book 3 in the Sneaky Inc. Spy Adventure

**CONTINUE
READING!**

The muse

The mad scientist

The writer

The soccer ninja

The horsey lover

Help support local authors
seeking to honor God in art
and business by offering
a _positive review_!

Thank you!

ALSO BY
Rob Baddorf

Christian Fiction!

I Fly Spaceships (Books 1-4)

Kimberly the Cat Series (Books 1-7)

Fighting Fear, Joshua 1:9 Series (Books 1-3)

A Sneaky Inc. Spy Adventure Series (Books 1-3)

Video Games Alive: Game, Die, Repeat.

Friday Night Monster Club

Armor of God Series

Raised by Summer

**Visit Rob Baddorf's
Amazon Author Page!**

instagram.com/
RobBaddorf

RobBaddorf.com

facebook.com/
RobBaddorfAuthor